Night to Dawn 37

I0517318

Illustrators:

Marge Simon: pages 16 and 49

Teresa Jay: back cover

Chris Friend: pages 32, 55, 56, 88, and 113

Sandy DeLuca: pages 13, 40, 78, and 104

Elizabeth Hattie Pierce-Collins: pages 3, 19, 72, and 103

Denny E. Marshall: pages 30, 60, 85, and 108

Sravani Singampalli: page 7

James Masters: pages 37, 38, 61, and 93

Night to Dawn No. 37, April, 2020, Copyright 2020 by Barbara Custer. All rights revert to individual author and artist after publication. ISSN # 1542-1430; ISBN: 978-1-937769-61-1

Night to Dawn is a semi-annual publication of fiction, poetry, artwork, articles, and review.

Orders, editorial, and queries: Barbara Custer, P. O. Box 643, Abington, PA 19001

Email: barbaracuster@hotmail.com or ntdsubmissions@gmail.com

PayPal orders: venus1021@juno.com.

Submissions: ntdsubmissions@gmail.com; Web: www.bloodredshadow.com

Pickings and Tidbits

Top of the balloon to y'all! ☺

As promised, I released Michael De Stefano's *Waiting for Grandfather*. There's been a delay on L. M. Labat's *The Sanguinarian Id: Schwartzwald*; however, I released Tom Johnson's *The Man in the Black Fedora*. I posted book covers and blurbs on the last page. Tom's book has netted several five-star reviews.

I have some sad news about Tom. He'd been struggling with his health during this past year, and he died November 5, 2019. I knew how sick he was, but I wanted him to see his book published. *The Man in the Black Fedora* will remain in print for the next three years, and I understand his other books will remain in print.

Rod Marsden has an upcoming release, *50 Dragons*, told in the late 23rd century. It depicts a society where everything appears heavenly, but is in fact, monstrous. His tale, "Second Thoughts," is a prologue to his book, which should go live in the early spring.

For *Night to Dawn 37*, I've introduced two new artists: James Masters and Sravani Singampalli. Teresa Jay did the illustration on the back cover. Alas, David Lowell Transue and Lonnie Weems have had health issues, so I've had no work from them to feature for this issue. Hope springs eternal for their recovery. Meantime, Sandy DeLuca, Marge Simon, Denny E. Marshall, Elizabeth Hattie Pierce, and Chris Friend have contributed many illustrations and poetry. By the by, I highly recommend you read Bryan Dietrich and Marge Simon's *The Demeter's Diaries*. They tell Dracula's story in alternating viewpoints between Mina and Vlad, in prose format. The verses kept me turning the pages, wondering if their love will realize consummation. Marge Simon's excerpts, "When Dracula Calls" and "Mina Senses Vlad at Whitby," will give you a delightful flavor of her tale.

Lee Clark Zumpe has contributed stories to chill you. "Blocula" describes a school for the unspeakable. In "The Sacrifice," a police officer pays the ultimate cost when he discovers the killer. Camping connotes fun, games, and romance. However, for one explorer, Zumpe's "Up the Finley Camp Prong" is death, where malevolent entities make zombie slaves out of the innocent.

In Harold Kempka's "Jerry's Emancipation," protag Jerry takes a lover, hoping to seek freedom from his domineering, late mother; but things don't exactly go as planned. David Harrington's "The Gravedigger" gives the occupational hazard of burying the dead, especially when the body isn't human. S. M. Bidwell's "Bead Trickling Laughter" belongs to a skeletal being that confronts the narrator as she tries to solve the mystery behind her sister's death. Margaret L. Carter's back with my two favorite lead characters, Roger and Britt, in "Werewolf Watch." The two doctors are hired to treat a human/werewolf hybrid who fears he's been attacking humans. And, speaking of beasts, watch out for the one in Linda Barrett's "The Black Dog of Newgrange;" his bite is worse than his bark.

A few weeks ago, I went to Lancaster, and inspired by Todd Hanks' "Snow Globe," I bought one that featured a Nativity scene. At first, I hesitated to buy because Todd's story came to mind, for the snow globe he describes is bewitched. Rajeev Bhargava's "Shadow Sheila" masquerades as a friend, but leads our lead character into a trap. A character in Christopher Dabrowski's story asks a question: "Excuse me, sir, is this a joke?" His reaction to aliens bent on world destruction is disbelief. Barry Yedvobnick 's "The Siren Lure" describes the results of an experiment gone horribly wrong. Francis-Marie de Châtillon's "The Doleful Tale of the Bucket of Blood" features an innocent-looking woman who carries around a bucket. Is she real, or is she a vengeful specter out to lure young men to their deaths? And what's in her bucket?

Night to dawn—a time when twilight melts into nightfall before the next day. Here, the line between life and death is often fuzzy. Dusk is a time when dead slither from their crypts. Our interactions take on an unnatural cast and the seams that hold our reality together split open. You might ask if the shadows that flit across the wall are reflections of the moonlight, or are they vengeful ghosts with unfinished business? In either case, twilight is a perfect time for *Night to Dawn*.

~ *Barbara* 😊 😊

Jerry's Emancipation
by
Hal Kempka

Jerry stood naked before the full-length mirror that had once hung on his mother's bedroom door. Tonight was going to be his first encounter with a woman since she died and only his third date ever. He held up several shirts, trying to decide what to wear on his blind date.

Hollow shadows rested where the whiteness of his skin sank into the depressions of his skeletal build. He glanced at his manhood and smiled, hoping that might make up for his otherwise less than manly appearance. *Boy, would Mother be pissed if she saw this,* he thought, smiling at his reflection.

Mother had always tended to his every need, and now he was on his own. He'd inherited her house, and the money he received from her investments and insurance would allow him to live modestly.

He had come to feel a lonely void in his life though and knew it was time to get out and live a little. Besides, he thought, Mother was gone now, and he wouldn't have to listen to her constant admonitions that women were evil and wrong for him. He wanted to find a woman to take care of him.

His date's name was Carla, and they'd met in an online singles website. While they lived in the same city, they texted and messaged each other for nearly a month before deciding to meet. Jerry hoped she wouldn't be disappointed, as he wasn't exactly how he'd represented himself in his profile.

For starters, his profile read that he lived in a condo, and was an on-the-go, beach-loving guy. The truth was, he did not have a condo and always lived at home with his mother. While he was an experienced swimmer, he certainly was not the lifeguard he proposed to be. He had, however, once saved a kitten from drowning in the huge birdbath Mother kept outside her kitchen window, and even performed CPR on it.

Jerry was also forty-one and balding, rather than his profile-stated age of twenty-six and a Photoshopped picture of him with a head of thick bushy hair.

He dressed and drove to Carla's house. After parking along the curb, he sat in his car, nervously smoking a cigarette. When he glanced at his reflection in the rearview mirror, Jerry flinched and spun around. He stared at the dark and empty back seat, sure he'd caught a glimpse of Mother staring at him from the darkened interior.

Mother certainly would not have approved, he thought and chuckled that he was defying her. After checking his breath, Jerry stepped from the car and walked toward the house. His stomach churned and his hands felt clammy.

When Jerry rapped on the door, it swung open immediately. A matronly looking woman wearing a brightly colored dress and heavy makeup stood before him, grinning ear to ear.

"Hello," Jerry said, "I'm Jerry, here to pick up Carla."

"Hi Jerry, I'm Carla," she said, appearing surprised. "Wow, you look just like you described yourself online."

He did a mild double-take and replied, "You, too."

Okay, he thought, he had it coming. Carla certainly wasn't the young cheerleader type she said she was. But she did look a lot like his mother and that felt comforting.

She grabbed her sweater, and Jerry escorted her to the car. They went to a movie and later stopped for a bite to eat. He found her as easy to talk to as his mother was, and he liked the way she fawned over him the entire evening, just like Mother had.

When they returned to her house, he awkwardly leaned over to kiss her cheek. Carla put a hand against his chest and pushed him back.

"Uh-uh, buddy. Not yet," she said.

"Oh, I'm sorry," Jerry said, his face flushing with embarrassment. "I didn't mean to be so forward. It's just that I had a wonderful time."

"Me too," she said. "But that's not why I stopped you."

"Well, why then?"

"Because I don't want the neighbors to see us out here. It's not right."

"Oh," he said. "I understand."

"Good, then come into the house with me, right now!" she commanded, cocking her head and flashing an elfish smile.

He followed her inside, content that she sounded just like Mother. Carla shut the door and turned to Jerry. Before he could say anything, she pulled him into the folds of her dress and held him tight. She couldn't keep her hands off him, and soon they were in the throes of passion.

Carla took control and demanded that they do everything her way, which Jerry didn't mind. She pampered him quite differently than the way his mother did, but oh, it felt so much better.

Jerry spent the night. The next morning, he walked to his car, rubber-legged and gratified to the point of dizziness. He spent the next two nights with her, and on the third night, Carla demanded that he move in so she could take care of him. Jerry obeyed, just as he always had with Mother, whom he never disobeyed.

On his drive home to retrieve his belongings, Jerry glanced at the back seat in his rearview mirror.

"Ha! Mother, I know you can hear me," he said, "and I know you promised you would always take care of me. But Carla is a wonderful girl, and I've decided to let her take care of me from now on. I hope you don't mind. You don't, do you, Mother?"

Jerry felt the car swerving to the left and shifted his glance toward the road. An eighteen-wheeler's lights blinded him as it plowed into him head-on. Jerry's car crumpled into a fiery casket of jumbled, melting metal, and the last he heard was his mother's demonic cackle over the semi's blaring horn.

The End

A Macabre Dream by Sravani Singampalli

Fireflies in their perilous eyes

Humongous their bodies

Behemoth in their demeanor

Tempestuous was the wind.

Wine-red were my tears

Crippled were their thoughts

Sprinting through the woods

Grisly things in my vicinity

Jeopardized my life.

Breaking free from monstrosity
Ashen-faced with cold feet
I became downhearted
Lost in the bizarre world.
I tried hard to escape
Those dark unfathomable eyes
My life became a spine-chilling tale
Howling sounds from behind.
Thunder in the sky seemed
Like temper tantrums
Of a frustrated old man.
The Behemoths still chasing
Their teeth like white daggers
Trying to taste
My cherry-red blood
At last clutched in their hands
Their fingers resembling
The pillar-like prop roots
Of a banyan tree.
I screeched hard with pain
My heart beating at the
Speed of a bullet train
I closed my eyes
Praying to god
To save my life
Reassured to discover my reality
As I opened my eyes.

After the Dawn by Matthew Wilson

Black Cape for sale
Slight tear and bloodstains
Nametag reads "Dracula."

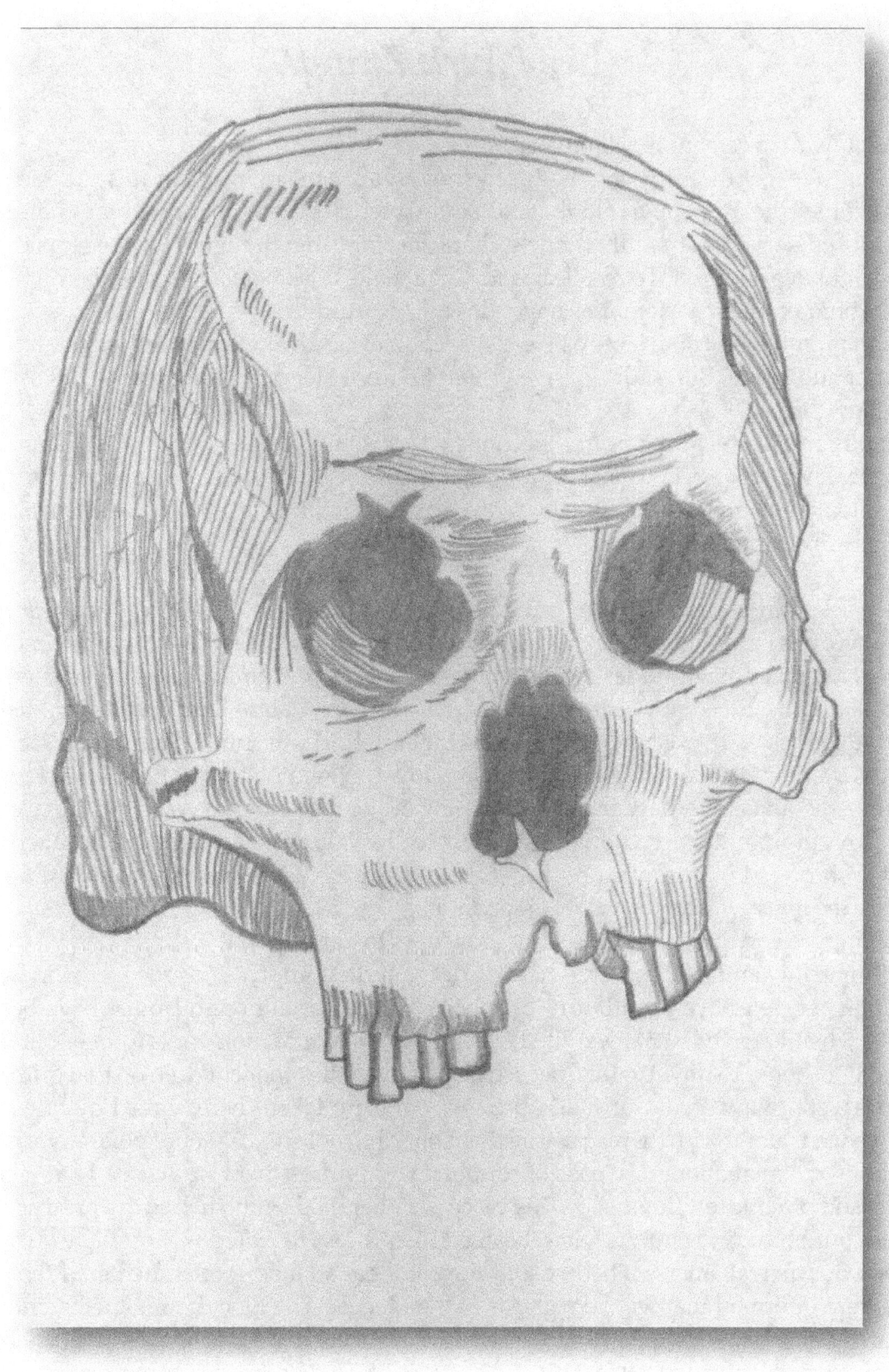

Blocula
by
Lee Clark Zumpe

I don't want to remember all the pain.

I want to forget the suffering, both physical and psychological, that this experience has put me through. I have heard people said that pain is an integral part of an individual's nature, and that agonies endured serve to strengthen one's character. Not this though. No one should have to go through what I have endured. To recollect is to relive the revulsion and to remember is to relinquish my tenuous hold on reality. Memories engender more torture.

Death might liberate me if only I were susceptible. Death alone has the potential to release me from thought and being. But, sadly, I haven't that luxury. The proverbial reaper has ostracized me from his fellowship.

Insanity might shield me from reflections which so frequently surface, but I am incapable of the blind weakness required to slip into such obscurity. Sometimes, for passing instants, I am propelled into an ephemeral dementia by more concentrated images, but my age has always foiled complete insanity. How I regret that.

Age.

My tracks can be traced through the decades, across several centuries. I have forgotten my exact birthdate, but I am confident in the claim that I arrived on this fetid earth sometime during the 17th Century. My parentage eludes me, and unquestionably my family line concludes with me. I do know that Dalecarlia, Sweden was my birthplace. It was here that my burden was molded, here that the infernal dealings were executed. Here it was that my soul was immortalized and sacrificed.

It was a tender meadow laced with crimson clover, extending farther than I could comprehend. Upon it lumbered a massive, dark mansion, looming out of the landscape with the same audacity of a cancerous growth upon tender young flesh. Framed by a ring-fence with a gate draped in various tones, and enshrouded in an ambiance not altogether as fresh as that which dominated the rest of the nearby fields, the house was an unavoidable spectacle.

The impure corruption of its posture drew eyes to gaze upon it.

This meadow and its ill-natured haven are the earliest impressions registered in my mind. In a sense, I may as well have been born—or reborn—there, for although I must have been in early adolescence when I arrived, whatever life I lived previous to that moment is forever buried.

I did not choose to travel to this place, nor did any of the other children on that grim campaign. Our parents were unaware of our fate, I believe. We were taken there, forced by faces unknown. Innocent, we went along with them, trusting them blindly, foolishly. No one spoke as we approached it; no one offered explanations or words of comfort. This impressment was carried out meticulously, and the parade of children flowing to this place was handled with such great precision it was as though both our abductors and we had rehearsed the process repeatedly.

Upon our arrival, after we had passed through that strange gate and entered the foreboding estate, we were informed that we were guests at the Blocula. The Blocula was the hereditament of a wealthy foreign prince. No name was advanced, and we were merely to address this prince as "Your Lordship" if ever we happened to meet him. We never did. This faceless prince had requested that several children be gathered from neighboring communities—bought or stolen—so that he might, through his apprentices, share his knowledge with us. We were told to think of our detention not as captivity, but as a privilege. We had been "enrolled in an institution of the highest learning, boasting ancient wisdom and towering morals." I recall those words quite clearly, as I recall the sardonic grin that erupted upon the speaker's face at their utterance.

And so began our schooling at the Blocula.

The curriculum our malnourished instructors preached was primary initially: Languages and numbers. Then, slowly, science, primarily biology, crept into the studies. History was discussed seldom, and when it was, it seemed to be concentrated predominately around plagues and wars. Our teachers seemed unwilling or unable to provide us with any substantial benefit humankind ever accomplished. Instead, they dwelt upon his ravaging crusades and conquests, and his tenacity toward external ideas and alien faiths.

To my knowledge, there were at least a hundred other children at the Blocula. We forged no friendships during our years there, for it was not permitted. There was an unspoken bond between us which kept us from developing any animosities; beyond that, we were detached. We also had no relationship with the teachers aside from our role as pupils. They were all skinny, pale ghost-like individuals ... some men, some women. They wore brown robes which licked the floor as they walked. A vacant dullness robbed their eyes of animation, and their voices buzzed a metered lament.

The mansion itself had a separate and discernible personality. Time altered its erratic moods, swinging it from one extreme to another. One day, the Blocula would be no less bright and pacific than the meadow outside; the following it would grow dark and enigmatic as if some ominous presence weighted the atmosphere. I distinctly recall that in specific passages, shadows would appear one day where there were none the previous day, and some chambers would become unseasonably cold or unbearably hot depending on the whim of the old lodge.

Three floors of this mad estate were accessible, readily available for exploration. Our custodians let us roam freely often; I guess they felt we were too insecure to attempt escape. The three levels held an incalculable number of rooms: Small, dank studies bloated with archaic volumes; barren, undecorated cubicles painted nauseating shades; vast auditoriums that reached for the outer limits of perception, populated by weird leering statues and accented with black draperies that banished the meadow.

And for every unlocked door in those three stories, there were two that were locked. I knew not how many more floors remained above, nor what cells might lie below.

Silence.

I remember that most of the Blocula ... silence, unearthly silence. The children rarely spoke, rarely cried, whined, or screamed. Even during and immediately after the abduction, none of us vented our fears or anger audibly. The instructors only conversed when they taught. None of the servants communicated. That alone made me apprehensive, made me curious and fearful of the true nature of the Blocula and the true intent of the mysterious foreign prince. A child's mind will wander if left unrestrained...

My mind did not need to wander far, for as time elapsed, the oddities of the mansion became more conspicuous. I only needed to peer into the benighted hallway during the twilight hours to uncover peculiarities. The staff would appear at sporadic intervals, sometimes wrapped in black cloaks, sometimes wholly undressed. They carried candles, hugged books beneath their arms, and held decanters from which thick black liquid would sometimes spill. They would enter the corridor from their rooms, then toward the front entrance they would walk. Strands of smoke hovered in the hallway like drooping, transparent banners. I had not a hint where they would go once outside the ponderous front doors, had not a clue what could draw them out into the cold night, until one night.

I alone abandoned the safety of the large hall where the majority of the children slept to steal into the shadows and pursue our hosts one grim night. I edged through the darkness to a suitable retreat where I might observe without being observed. It was in a library on the ground floor, one of the few rooms that afforded a generous view of the front lawn. Outside, I could see a number of our teachers, though their ever-featureless faces hindered absolute identification. With them, several others had gathered, mostly females. They sat or stood in the lawn, all eyes affixed to a moderate fire, flames burning orange and red.

And in the fire, there was a face.

It was not a human face, not a face of flesh, but still, it was a face. It did not speak, but I thought I could feel its eyes move about, searching for understanding, for loyalty, and faith.

The sky lacked stars or moon, that eve; it was a purple veil suspended. The grounds were unnatural, the vegetation rigid and pale. Only from the fire came light, and the circle it provided stretched only to the front gate. Just outside, I detected movement, a constant waving motion from left to right ... no single forms were apparent, just a continual sweeping action.

The gates opened soon, and from the void came a parade of older people, naked save for their wrinkled shells, marching toward the fire. At a painfully lethargic gait, they drew up to the flame. Thirteen in all, I counted, circling the face, circling the fire. The eyes of the congregation were affixed to this company ringing the inferno and reacted as the fire flared higher and higher as the procession circled repeatedly. As it became more intense, many of the teachers and visitors were forced to relocate. The radius of illumination grew accordingly, so that much of the field outside the gate became visible. The motion I detected earlier was now unveiled: A floating river of red, perhaps blood, surged through the air a short measure above the ground, endlessly flowing.

I noticed then, too, that the sky above was indeed vacant of celestial objects as I had before perceived, but not due to thick, hanging clouds as I had guessed. As I peered upward, I beheld hordes of winged demons filling the air and disfiguring the heavens above the Blocula. So many had taken wing that the sun might have burned aloft and it still would have been black beneath.

I felt meaningless, impossibly small. Fear seeped from my pores and fastened me to the floor. Their numbers alone overwhelmed me, but the numbing horror of those misshapen brethren of Hell that swarmed overhead shall haunt me for all eternity. As I watched, the thirteen elderly participants ended their circular promenade around the flames. They stopped, turned toward it, and walked calmly into the face, into the fire.

The blaze remained intense, and the demons began diving from their aerial arena, swooping down and landing in the yard. I finally fled from the library, dashed back to the sleeping hall and into my bed, entombing myself beneath a heavy comforter. I think it was their voices I heard after retreating to my bunk. Laying there, longing for sleep to come to shelter me, I forced myself to listen. I heard high-pitched, whistling noises that seemed to form words or ideas. I could also hear the human voices of the teachers, laughing and conversing.

That was the only time I ever saw demons, to my knowledge. The curriculum at Blocula changed steadily and rapidly after that evening. We all became quite adept in medicine; many of us developed speaking skills which would have put Socrates to shame. Some were taught the intricacies of religions. And some, I recall, were instructed in much darker arts...

And others yet, I also recall, vanished from the Blocula.

The years piled up, and I matured into a young man at the Blocula. When I was in my mid-twenties, the number of students had dwindled from over one hundred to thirteen. What happened to the others I will never know. What I had come to accept by this time was that my life was not normal. I realized that I had been chosen for some pursuit not common nor well-known. In that sense, I was proud. I also deduced that my teachers, my keepers, were not welcomed by the outside world and that I would not be welcome when and if I left the sanctuary.

But then, on the eve of St. Walpurgis' Day one year, we were summoned into the meadow. We were told to gather our meager belongings for we would soon be leaving the Blocula, and we would not be allowed to return until "called home."

It was 1694.

Outside, we gathered around a fire, not unlike the one I had beheld years before. A face stared out from the pit of the inferno, cold and powerful. One of the instructors approached us, holding forward a sizable tome and a quill. He asked us each to prick a finger with the instrument, then sign our names in the text with blood as ink. We consented without thought. As the last of us laid his signature, the skies spilled a deluge upon us, though the stars were visible, and no clouds occupied the night air. The rain had a reddish tint about it and was accompanied by a sour scent. It lasted only briefly.

Next, our instructors threw the filings of clocks into a vat of water and recited: "As these filing of the clock do never return to the clock from which they are taken, so may my soul never return to the Blocula until summoned." We repeated this dutifully. A feast followed this, served by the servants and educators of the Blocula. The amount of food offered was ludicrous, as a continual ribbon of people bearing plates and bowls rippled from the door of the mansion. As we ate, the masters of the Blocula delivered their last discourse and depicted the purpose of our existences. It was a mindless purpose. We had little work to do for everything would come naturally.

And so it was then we learned what we had become. We thirteen people, men and women, had been selected to eat the souls of all the damned on earth.

"Before us stands the Chosen, the Thirteen Vessels who shall serve our Lord for the ensuing Age. Behind us now is the brief period of clemency that He kindly granted humanity." The words rolled across the meadows and were whispered by things unseen in the darkness beyond. "Let the despots and tempters, the defilers and cannibals know that their damnation will once more be welcomed. The Gates of Hell await!"

We were commissioned officers of that foreign prince and had earned the honor of being His soul-ingestors. We serve this world and His realm, by devouring, consuming, and storing all those rancid souls destined for Hell.

It was further explained, that we might see some rationale in our task. Hell, we were informed, can only open its gates to new arrivals once every five centuries. Until then, all those souls marked for eternal damnation must be held in a temporal state on earth. And the only vessel which can contain a soul in this world is living flesh. And so, each of these spirits is dragged into one of us at death. We act like spiritual magnets for the condemned.

Like the lowly worms which swallow the vacant shells of humanity, so we gorge ourselves on the ill essence of the profane.

The horror of that instant of discovery could not compare to that which awaited us. We were not told of the side-effects. We were not told that each time a soul enters us, we feel their sins, their pain, and their death. We may be practically immortal, but we've each died a million times.

Our service began days later. We were granted some interim of peace, a delay before the inundation of souls commenced. We went our separate ways, some to Asia, others to Europe.

I was already making my way to the New World when I experienced my first episode. I cannot shake that memory ... that first time seemed to last forever ... darkness, like fainting, only consciousness unfortunately lingered. Then, a fast heavyweight crushed in on my chest while simultaneously, my lungs swelled so much they felt like they'd burst. Finally, the images started. The sins. All the evil fabric that comprised that soul, the vile threads which held it together. The deeds played out in my mind, so vivid I could taste the emotions. A protracted segment of eternity, I thought, had passed. But it was only an instant, not even a fraction of a second.

I grew used to it over time. As long as I don't think about it, as long as I remember to close my mind to the incoming images, it no longer troubles me. If I hadn't adapted, I don't know what I would have done.

Initially, I tried to commit suicide.

It was that same day; I was still traveling in a wagon caravan toward Stockholm. I had eaten many souls during that day, perhaps forty. I made the decision that I could not function while these accursed wraiths pelted me with their repulsive malignancy. As I sat in a carriage, I raised a small utility knife with stolid volition, sank it into my wrist where the blue vein slept beneath the skin and pulled it slowly up my arm. The other two passengers slept through my futile attempt at suicide and the ensuing miraculous recovery. Though the gash ran the length of my forearm, it wept no blood. The flesh repaired itself almost instantly.

Thankfully, I was able to develop barriers to shield myself from the average battery of immorality. With time, I was able to deal with my curse. Yet, no matter how well-buffered I may be, there are still conditions in which I lose my composure. Of course, considering the population of these recent centuries and the vast number of lives expiring each day due to wars and plagues and famine, it seems that very few are committed to the retribution mortals call Hell. I rarely devour more than four hundred souls a day, and nearly all of these are easily screened so that I am not traumatized. But with the painless hundreds, occasionally comes a soul so loathsome and fetid that I am wounded by its ingress.

Some such extremely degenerate beings are known widely for their evil. Locked within me are the tainted spirits of Hermann Mudgett, America's first serial killer; Adolfo De Jesus Constanzo; and Ed Gein. Still others have committed similar or worse abominations, but were never recognized by society and thus not punished. They shall be, though, soon enough. If only I might summon the strength to reveal to the oblivious masses the hidden horrors that our earthly kinsman practice behind stony walls of ageless citadels ... such offenses produced in the name of Beings far more venomous than even His Lordship, He that I unwittingly was reared to serve.

Centuries have passed since I left the Blocula. I have moved from country to country, continent to continent. I have lived many different lives.

I know at least my final destiny. I and the others will someday be called to return to the Blocula. We will circle the fire in the meadow until it ignites the air. Then we will pass into the flames, taking with us a flock of banished souls.

How I long to see the crimson clover of the Blocula.

Afterward

In 1669, eighty-five persons, including fifteen children, were burned to death after the Royal Commission of King Charles XI found them guilty of being practicing witches. The *Mora Witches* were accused of seducing hundreds of children into flying to the Blocula, which was described as "a large, delicate meadow, of which you can see no end. The place or house they met at had before it a gate painted with diverse colors." Though many made confessions, the location of the Blocula was never determined, and many children were never found.

Aberrant Artifacts Found in Two Owl Indian Mound by Lee Clark Zumpe

Amidst marlberry trees and cabbage palms
where Two Owl Creek
feeds the Manatee River,
long shadows stretch across the sandy shore.

Horseshoe-shaped shell middens roll
against the curving sweep
of flood waters,
as clouds hover over Tampa Bay.

Some relics do not bow to history:
Atypical objects too often
find themselves
relegated to museum closets.

I stand upon the temple mound,
the ghosts of great chiefs
pinned to my soul
while the moon wavers timidly.

Pottery shards, bones, and fetishes:
I know the secret names
of ancient gods worshipped
amidst marlberry trees and cabbage palms.

Mina Senses Vlad's Arrival at Whitby*
by
Marge Simon

This morning at breakfast, I forced myself to eat a scone, heaping it with strawberry jam. I knew Father was watching me. He folded his napkin, smiling at me. "Pleased to see you're looking well today, my dear. It appears that I'm to make a brief jaunt to Darbyville to discuss the sale of some property we can do without. Would you like to accompany me there? The shops are quaint and offer bobbles women like. I think you will enjoy perusing them while I meet with Mr. Brace-girdle."

Indeed, I was overjoyed for a release from these walls. As the carriage jogged along, Father reached over to take my hands. "I'm most pleased you came with me, my dear," he said. "This business about Jonathan's absence — not to mention his lack of communication — has disturbed us all." He looked closely at my face. "I'm aware that your malaise is caused by deep concern for your intended. It breaks my heart that I cannot provide any answers." He went on to explain that his inquiries about Jonathan had been to no avail. He'd thought perhaps Jonathan's ship had foundered en route back. He did find mention of a missing vessel, The Demeter. Apparently, it had not yet arrived on schedule. A recent sighting of it by French sailors was the only thing on record. Curiously, it had strayed from its original course, but the sails were at full furl, and nothing about it seemed amiss. It was assumed that the captain had received a change of orders at some port en route.

My One, I wasn't even thinking about Jonathan while he spoke. We drove on in silence until something very odd happened. A sudden burst of lightning split the skies all around our carriage. It was inexplicable, for the bolts came straight out of a cloudless blue sky! The horses spooked and the carriage bounced around, half on and half off the road. I must have hit my head on the window frame because I can't remember a thing until I awoke on a settee. Father was administering smelling salts. A sweet old lady hovered near, and once I was awake, insisted I take a sip of brandy as a restorative. My temple was sore, but I assured them both I was feeling better and urged him to continue with his business.

Outside, I sensed Your salty breath upon the wind, by far a more restorative than brandy. Had I my way, I'd take the carriage onward to the sea. I crave something new, something more powerful. The taste of blood on my tongue. You.

The End

*(extract from *The Demeter Diaries*, with Bryan Dietrich, Independent Legions)

When Dracula Calls*
by
Marge Simon

Do You whisper my name? But I know you *did*! This night I felt compelled to find you, to speak to You. Rising from my bed and drawing on my robe, I tiptoed downstairs to the patio. The evening was humid, heavy with perfume of lilac and honeysuckle.

Jonathan always brings a bouquet for me when he visits, but even the sweetest flowers lose their scent so quickly, or so it has seemed in recent days. What flower would You select for me?

Perhaps this part is from a dream or perhaps I confuse my real world with another, but I saw a shaft of moonlight cutting a swath through the garden. At its end, there was a single blood rose, strangely open this late and in full bloom. Drawn to its fragrance, I held its stem. Feeling a sharp prick, I drew back quickly. My thumb was wet with blood and I saw its thorns were grown huge, almost as big as the rose itself! Just as I turned to go inside, I heard the flapping of wings. So near they came, I felt the wind of their passage. I supposed it was some huge bird of darkness.

It feels so right to linger here. The trees are silhouetted below a gibbous moon. Such quietude, now I can almost hear your thoughts, and your desires must be mine as well.

The End
*(extract from *The Demeter Diaries*, with Bryan Dietrich, Independent Legions)

Composite Nightmare by Marc Shapiro

I can hear it
Dreaded monster of the mind
Made of nuts and bolts
And last night's dinner
Closer
Closer
On cloven feet
Flowered in overripe bane
And nourished by ruptured jugular
Under my door
Over my bed
It won't bite
It isn't real
Or is it?

The Gravedigger
by
David B. Harrington

My name is Shywood Green and I'm a gravedigger. I'm the guy they refer to in my business as "The Finisher." I'm the first one to come and the last one to go when all the mourners have gone home to grieve. In my twenty plus years on the job, I've seen it all, from corpses sitting up in their caskets to wild dogs digging up fresh graves and everything in between. At 6'2", 225 pounds, it takes a lot to rattle my nerves. But nothing could have prepared me for what happened on that cold and foggy night in early November.

It was right around quitting time, and I was just finishing up for the day. Temperatures were dropping fast, and Saint Alban's Cemetery was silent and still. It was getting dark and Willy, the backhoe operator, had already gone home for the weekend. I was working feverishly, putting the finishing touches on a grave we had dug earlier that morning, getting it ready for the marble head-stone due to be delivered and set in place in three days. The body belonged to one Veronica Black-stone, a mysterious young widow allegedly involved with the occult who had evidently died under some rather dubious circumstances just days before. I remembered hearing the rumors circulating around town, something about the young widow being responsible for the recent disappearances of several schoolchildren from the local parish. At the time, I really didn't believe a word of it; they were, after all, just rumors.

I could barely make out the silhouette of the old church and the crumbling tombstones; the fog was so thick. My fingers and toes were tingly and numb from working all day in the bitter cold. I sat down on a nearby tombstone, smoking and rubbing my hands together, when I heard a faint scratching noise coming from the widow's grave. It sounded like a raccoon or something clawing in the dirt. I took a flashlight from the Ditch Witch and went over to investigate. I slowly tiptoed around to the other side of the mound, but didn't see anything. No raccoon, no scratch marks, no nothing. I got down on my hands and knees on the half-frozen ground and pressed my ear against the grave. The scratching was coming from inside. Could rats or mice have chewed their way through the casket already? Or had we inadvertently buried the young widow alive? I slowly backed away from the grave. It gave me the chills. I tried to shake it off and convince myself that it was just my imagination playing tricks on me. I was fatigued. It had been a long day and I was anxious to get home. I packed up my stuff and got ready to leave when I looked over and noticed a peculiar red mist rise up from the widow's grave, swirling around in the fog like a floating pool of blood. Slowly the figure of a woman began to take shape. Blurred features formed on her face: A pointed nose, a crooked grin, and a pair of sunken eye sockets staring blankly into the darkness. The specter called out to me from another dimension, softly whispering my name over and over, "*Sshyywood… Sshyywood…*"

An uneasy feeling of despair followed me all the way home. Inside, the house was cold and dark. I cranked up the heat, crawled into bed, and slowly drifted off. The phantom lady stayed with me all through the night, pursuing me in my sleep, haunting my dreams and whispering my name over and over, "*Sshyywood… Sshyywood…*" I must have tossed and turned for a good part of the evening because at 1:00 a.m., I suddenly woke up shivering in a cold sweat and sat straight up in bed. Trembling with trepidation, I bundled myself up in blankets and cautiously made my way downstairs. The house was dark and quiet. Outside the fog was dense, a light steady breeze was blowing, and the ground was coated with a fresh layer of frost.

I was alone in the house, or so I thought. The bedroom door clicked shut. Then I heard the familiar scratching sounds coming from the bedroom and the phantom lady's desperate cries as she whispered my name repeatedly, "*Ssshyyywood … Ssshyyywood…*" I knew what I had to do. I grabbed my coat and hurried back to the cemetery. I climbed the twisting path through the darkness until I reached the widow's grave at the top of the grassy hill and started doing what I do best.

For what seemed like an eternity, I dug and dug, and didn't stop digging until I found the casket three hours later. I threw my shovel aside, got down on all fours, and cleared away the remaining soil. I picked up my crowbar and pried as hard as I could. After several attempts, the lid gave way and flung open. I was appalled by what I saw. Or more precisely, what I didn't see. For the body of the young woman whom I thought we had accidentally buried alive was gone. All that remained was her empty casket. Horrified and confused, I stood up when something as light as a feather gently brushed against my shoulder. "*Ssshyyywood…Ssshyyywood…*" I whirled around and there she was, just hovering in the freezing fog like a relentless ghostly apparition pleading to be set free. She stretched out her hand and I recoiled instinctively. I stumbled backwards, tripped over my shovel, and into the casket I tumbled. The lid slammed shut. I was trapped. I banged and kicked as hard as I could, but no matter how hard I tried, the lid refused to give way. From above I heard the sound I had been dreading the most: The first shovelful of dirt coming down on top of me. Then another, and another. I kicked and kicked and slammed my body up against the lid over and over, but it was just no use. I had to find a way out and fast, otherwise I would end up buried alive and nobody would ever know. In desperation, I bent my knees as far as they could go, and using both my feet, kicked the side of the casket with all my might. The casket split apart, splintering into pieces, and dirt started cascading in. I slid through the narrow opening and crawled up out of the grave. I looked around but there was nobody there. My shovel still lay on the ground right where I had tossed it moments before.

For the next two hours, I worked feverishly filling in the widow's empty grave and smoothing out the soil. By the time I finally finished, the first morning light was beginning to glow on the horizon. I quickly gathered up my things and ran from the cemetery. I never spoke a word to anyone about my frightening encounter with the crimson lady that cold and foggy November night. Sometimes late at night when I'm sleeping, I can still hear her calling to me from beyond the grave, softly whispering my name over and over, "*Sshyywood...Sshyywood...*"

The End

Slaves of Evil Queens by Matthew Wilson

I have stormed the monster's castle
the villain who has cursed the lands
setting fire to my parents' village
who laughed at times brief sounds.

Through the ebon hallways I wandered
past flags made of human skin
prisons swollen with failed heroes
shallow graves that home my kin.

In the perfumed throne room, I found her
glowing in a red light of devotions
drinking from her diamond goblets
a sweet crimson to fill all oceans.

Her eyes promised immortality
the seduction of that angelic beast
who tore my throat and sang to me
and for 1000 years showed me how to feast.

Sacrifice
by
Lee Clark Zumpe

RED, BLUE, BROWN.

Sickly, burnt red flecked over lips and chin and painted into tendrils which stretched listlessly down over naked breast. Red so solid that it could be read from the teeth upon which it had hardened. So vivid Benny could feel it tarnishing the inside of her throat.

And that shade of blue; he had seen it a hundred times. It was a color that no rainbow would ever unfurl, no set of children's crayons would ever contain. So garish that he no longer felt it could be called "blue:" How could the absence of life be related by simple color?

This grisly portrait was marginally offset by the brown shag carpet upon which the victim was splayed. Being a light brown, the rug would have displayed earnestly supplementary speckles of red had the artist wished it so. But no. The painting was subtle in its account.

Benny flipped through all the different vantage points of the same picture. Each glossy photo strung out the same set of colors, the same blood, the same lifeless flesh. Benny longed for the days of black and white. The colors seemed to act as transponders, emitting pulses. He imagined fear and pain. Was fear red, or pain blue?

Much about the scene in the pictures disturbed Benny. More than just the colors. The way the body lay bothered him. It wasn't that it was unnatural; that's what he would expect from a murder or even a suicide. It was actually too natural, too comfortable looking. The body didn't reveal much about how it had come to such a tragic state.

Certainly, the face was contorted and disturbed; the eyes were wide with fright or madness. The mouth was gaping, teeth bared like a slavering and ravenous hound.

Benny had had enough of the puzzle for one day. He closed the file folder and stuffed it haphazardly into the drawer of his desk, simultaneously groping for the keys in his pants pocket. He would retreat from the office, and he would try to leave the mystery behind. But the case was more difficult to abandon than his desk.

Traveling across the Bayway, Benny's mind continued to focus on the Polaroid photos. Pictures captured the details but left out the image. Being there was something altogether different. It was still clear, the morning he walked up to 2222 Rosetree Lane. Even after half a dozen homicide detectives and medical examiners had sifted through the house, even after the journalists had swooped down for the scoop, the place was still charged. Static. The hunger had seeped into the furniture, the walls, the knick-knacks. It might not have stained the brown shag, but it was down there nonetheless. He could feel it squish beneath his wingtips. He smelled the scent of it on the air. No one else could.

Benny watched the sun set over the barrier islands from the vacant lot of a new subdivision. From a takeout box on the dash, he finger-fed himself kung-pao chicken. MSG made his tongue tingle. The radio offered up fuzzy jazz while he sipped cold tea.

Warm blood.

Whoever did it, whoever committed this atrocity apparently liked blood. The coroner's report was quick to point it out. Blood had been drained from the victim's tongue.

The press would cry "Vampire Killer" if word got out. They would be wrong. Benny had seen the havoc left behind by so-called vampires. There was a considerable corpus readily available to law enforcement agencies covering the Matamoros cult killings; the Solis case from Monterrey, Mexico; even the Nosferatu-faced Chikatilo cannibal of Russia.

And of course, the Santa Cruz incident was still fresh in his mind.

Vampire killers, serial killers, were messy. Prone to cannibalism, mutilation, necrophilia. Most of them fell into fairly strict demographic borders. There were exceptions, but few.

There were blood fetishists, too. They ran the gamut of TV talk shows, some too eccentric to believe, others rather sincere in an uncomfortable sort of way. They rarely indulged in their habit without total consent.

Benny eyed his Colt Diamondback at rest in the passenger seat. He had no silver bullets. But then, they only worked on werewolves anyway. He put his faith in the .38 Special, and in the Ithica Mag-10 Roadblocker he kept in the trunk. He would call upon the aid of one or the other before this was over. His intuition was telling him that the perpetrator of this crime would never come to trial; he would never be taken into custody alive.

The sun was gone. His takeout box was empty, except for discarded water chestnuts. His fingers felt around the floor, through stacks of bulging manila folders, dancing over wadded up burger wrappers, looking for his fortune cookie. Wrapped in plastic.

"*It* requires more courage to suffer than to die."

Benny smiled. He didn't know Napoleon was Chinese.

Morning was a tease. He waited long for it, growing tired of looking at spots on his ceiling, tired of listening to his neighbor snore through inadequate apartment paper-thin walls. Sleep offered him only more reds, more blues, more browns. Naked blue.

There was some evidence suggesting a sexual assault. Minor abrasions on the wall of the vagina. No trace of semen. No extraneous pubic hair. The coroner mentioned the possibility that a miscarriage had occurred within the last thirty days. Again, the medical evidence pointed weakly in that direction but seemed insufficient.

The coroner was embarrassed to report some of his findings. He couldn't really resolve any of the inconsistencies he dug up. What implement had been used to make fourteen almost undetectable punctures in her mid-section? Considering the location of the incision which opened her tongue, why wasn't her jaw dislocated or broken?

****

"I think we should call the FBI in on this."

"What for?" Benny asked. He hadn't shaved; his lack of sleep revealed itself in the red-purple semi-circles which dangled beneath his eyes. The chief reprimanded him with a cold stare. Too soon they would give up on this one. They didn't want to dirty themselves with the prospect of failure. "I can handle the case."

"We could have a serial killer here. I think we should let their profiling team have a look." Chief Stoner never liked these cases. Blood bothered him, especially when it was missing.

"Yeah, maybe." A cigarette bobbed across his lip; smoke curled into the air and faded. "Maybe you should have more faith."

"They got another one. Down in south county. Sounds like the same MO to me. Lady's got a chunk of her tongue missing."

"Really." Benny had been around longer than his superior. "How many channels carried the story last night, boss?"

"It leaked," he said, disgusted. "Doesn't mean this is a copycat though." Stoner tried to level out his anxiousness. "Get out there, look around. Call me."

Benny took the lead and spent the morning investigating a domestic violence call that was at a tangent to his case. As it turned out, a crack addict had come home and found his girlfriend screwing a neighbor in his bed. After running the guy off, he assaulted her in a manner that mimicked the lead story on the 11:00 news. First, he beat her until she was unconscious; then he used a hole punch to mutilate her tongue. During his call to 911, he reported the crime and claimed that the vampire killer had murdered his girlfriend. She was still unconscious when the police arrived. Though she had lost a considerable amount of blood and her wounds were critical, the paramedics told Benny's fellow officers that she would survive.

Benny didn't bother reporting back in. By taking the time to check out what he knew would be a copycat crime, he had allowed Chief Stoner enough time to shuffle an adequate number of papers to get the Feds excited. Going back to the cop shop might mean being yanked off the case. Keeping his mouth shut for an afternoon might earn him a real lead.

****

"Don't matter s'much to me as to thems over in Eastside," said Ninth Street Harry. Benny stooped down and followed the derelict into his living room beneath the I-10 overpass. "I ain't seen nuth'n over this a'way, boss, but I's heard stories."

"What kind of stories have you heard, Harry?" Benny had known Harry for years. He was a dingy, sour-smelling, toothless old man. Harry was pale and dirty, with big blue eyes focusing on something distant and unattainable, and with gray grandfather curls ringing his head like a crown. He was respected among the homeless, not like a king but as an elder. Didn't know where he came from. Couldn't remember his full name. Once, Benny tried to help Harry discover his past but came up empty-handed. "Tell me what you've heard."

"This 'bout 'dat damn plague, ain't it, boss? Yeah, I's heard 'bout 'dat plague makin' lotsa folks over Eastside sick. Lotsa folks done died on the street in the night."

"I haven't heard of any epidemic in the inner-city ... how many people?"

"Can't say 'dat I know ... but I'll tells ya what got 'em sick. Its 'em damn rats!"

"Rats?"

"Yessir, jes like your Black Death it is, 'em rats is carrying some kinda disease ... its makin' people git sick. Lotsa folks got bit and whatnot."

Ninth Street Harry eased himself down on an olive-green sofa cushion which was probably his bed. There were a few empty bottles strewn around, newspapers, empty Green Giant cans, three pairs of sunglasses, a spare pair of shoes (which were far too large for Harry's feet), and a small television with a shattered tube. Harry coughed, wiped his nose on his sleeve. His lips were puffy and split. "Some says 'em rats stand right ups on dey hind legs. Whattya think a' dat boss, on dey hind legs!"

****

Benny didn't put much effort into researching Harry's wild ramblings. He figured the old dreg was finally cracking up completely. On a whim, however, he did push an inquiry through downtown requesting information on unusual illnesses cropping up in hospitals and walk-in clinics on the Eastside.

The response was disappointing in a way, but it was the one Benny had expected: Aside from sporadic cases of the flu, no contagious diseases have been reported in the past four months in the metropolitan area. Not even a kid with chickenpox.

****

Weeks dragged by. Benny's age seemed to progress exponentially. Since taking on the case four months back, gray hairs had begun colonizing his temples, his brow looked like shattered marble, and he'd lost fourteen pounds.

It was fashionable to believe that to catch a monster, you had to become one. Benny felt like he was spiraling back down the chain of evolution, becoming a frustrated animal stalking elusive prey.

Since the original incident on Rosetree, there had been two additional murders that were unquestionably the work of the same killer. The MO was the same, without even a minor deviation. The medical examiners came to the same distressing conclusions they had reached before: There were more things about the corpses that they couldn't explain than things they understood.

Much to Benny's amazement, Stoner had held off on sending the FBI invitations to their grisly little party. The chief had come across an ounce of self-respect tucked away in the recesses of his soul. For once, he wasn't too keen on letting the glory of the collar slip away. His unrestrained resolve, unfortunately, caused him to hound Benny. He pushed the veteran cop relentlessly, calling him at home in the middle of the night with his out-of-the-box theories, and insisting on tagging along with him on visits to crime scenes.

It was quiet the next week.

Instead of welcoming the break, Benny began to wonder if the killer had left the area. What if the killer was still killing, murdering victims in another city? How would he know ... how could he help bring an end to the terror? He had no practical way of accessing records in other states to check for similar cases.

The FBI had that capability.

Feeling utterly defeated, he had to admit that the time had come to call in the Feds.

He told Stoner to alert the FBI on a Monday morning. Stoner, in an abrupt and tense voice, informed him he had already done so Friday afternoon. They would be arriving by noon.

There came the obligatory briefing, when Feds met with the Sgt. Friday's of the world. It was always uncomfortable, sometimes hostile. Benny felt as though the Bureau always came in with a predetermined attitude; they were the parents who had been called down to school to clean up their kid's mess. They never said it, but Benny got the impression they were thinking *Well, there wouldn't be a serial killer loose if you had done your jobs and caught this guy after the first murder.*

"I noticed that forensics on the victims is pretty sketchy, and that's at its best." The one that did the talking was a young man with a fair complexion and short blond hair. His posture and demeanor suggested that he came from a wealthy, New England family. His older stoic partner, whose terminal grimace prompted Benny to grin at him obnoxiously, could've passed for Johnny Cash's twin brother. "I'd like to bring in someone from Quantico to reexamine the bodies."

"That's your prerogative, sir." Stoner smiled and nodded. He had shifted gears again and was now wholly engaged in making an ass of himself. He excelled in that field. It made Benny sick. "We'll make sure that you have everything you could possibly want."

Except the killer, thought Benny.

Benny bowed out eagerly as soon as the Feds were ready to move ahead with their investigation. He agreed unequivocally that the FBI had to be brought in; but, deep inside, he knew instinctively that they would fare no better on this case than he.

Walking through the precinct, he happened to overhear two officers discussing their most recent arrest. It seemed that a fairly respectable dentist had tried to kill one of his patients while she was undergoing a root canal. The report showed that a hygienist ran from the room, screaming and hysterical; when another employee went in, she found the dentist squatting on the victim drilling directly into her throat.

Benny shook his head and went home for the day.

****

Two weeks later, on a Wednesday afternoon—approximately two months since the Rosetree murder—the interim of peace came to an abrupt end.

In one afternoon, six more murders were reported. The Bureau was so overloaded checking out all the different crime scenes that they tapped Benny to work the sixth. He had been keeping an eye on the Feds' investigation, and he hadn't been overly impressed. He jumped at the chance to return to the mystery.

When he arrived, he found something he hadn't expected: A survivor.

Paramedics were working frantically and glared at Benny when he strolled into the small apartment. Tubes snaked up the victim's arms and burrowed beneath her pale skin. Her lips had already taken on the garish blue tone; her eyes darted about wildly. Needles plunged into her veins as strangers struggled to keep her alive.

Benny was shoved against a wall in the commotion. He had great difficulty staying out of the way in the tiny living room. He finally sank down in a ragged old recliner and watched.

He saw her, saw that she was conscious. The paramedics spoke to her; she shook her head once. She whispered something to them. She seemed cognizant.

He just wanted to ask one question, one question and they could take her off to the hospital, and he wouldn't bother her again until he'd gotten the okay from Surgeon General.

He squatted down on the floor, careful not to disturb the paramedics. His face was only inches away from hers.

He flashed his badge; she saw it glimmer and she looked at him.

"Who?" was all he said.

Her response made no sense. Still, he didn't discount it completely. There were too few leads for that.

She said, simply, "Inside."

****

The ninth victim died on the way to the hospital. Benny paced around the apartment, pointing here and there indicating what he wanted photographed. Flashbulbs blinded him.

He wandered off into the bedroom while others dusted for prints. The wall switch failed to illuminate the darkened room, so he was forced to use the weak pen-sized flashlight he carried. His eyes followed its circle of light as it swept around the room.

Something moved.

He strained his eyes, narrowed the beam of his light, and moved forward a little. His right hand sought his holster.

Whatever it was, it was huddled beneath a blanket on the floor. Its breathing was heavy and shallow and fast. It was small, too small to be an adult. It shuddered and gasped.

Though its outline was clearly defined under his flashlight, Benny couldn't quite identify it yet ... was it a child? A dog?

A rat?

He whipped back the blanket and a cat hissed at him.

Relief swept over him.

When he knelt to pet the cat, he felt something warm and sticky. The cat squirmed and howled in agony. His fingers wrapped about its neck, sinking into a deep gash in its throat. Something had cut it open.

Or, something had bitten it.

"George!" he cried out to a colleague, "Get your boys in here .... NOW!"

****

Benny sat on Ninth Street Harry's green sofa cushion. There was no sign of the old recluse. It looked as though he had not been around for weeks. In fact, there were very few homeless people down there. The grocery carts were gone; the refrigerator boxes were empty and abandoned. He had stopped at the mission earlier and found only a handful of beggars.

The sky was dusk purple. Orange wisps set sail from the Pacific inland. Cars raced by overhead on I-10.

One killer couldn't have committed six murders in four hours over an area of sixty square miles. The FBI decided that they were dealing with a cult. Somebody even suggested that it could be some kind of Manson revival. Maybe the family had returned, better organized and more efficient, and Charlie was guiding them from behind bars.

Benny watched as a figure shambled down the sidewalk toward him.

As he drew closer, Benny shifted his weight so he could defend himself more effectively.

"You're that cop ... lookin' for Harry?"

"Yeah," Benny answered. "You seen him?"

"Nah. I think they got him."

"Who?"

"You know — the rats."

"He got sick?" Benny looked at him curiously.

"No." The man's haggard face wrinkled up with frustration, and he made fists of his hands. "I mean, the rats got him."

"You mean the rats from the Eastside?"

"Yeah, but they're running out of food over there. They've been moving this way." The man then became anxious and fearful, his expression changing to reflect his apprehension. He looked around, eyeing the shadows beneath the overpass. Darkness was endemic outside of the streetlights; night had fallen.

"Look," Benny got to his feet. He tried to calm the homeless man by clutching his shoulder gently, but it only frightened him more. "Can you just tell me where Harry is?"

"In the sewers, I suppose," he said, fidgeting and stuttering now. He started to move away from Benny, continuing on his way at a slightly faster pace. "They always take people down there." He shuffled away, shunning the shadows and calling back to Benny, "I've got to go, got to get to the mission."

Benny watched him a while, watched how he clung to the circles of light beneath the streetlamps. He gave the sewer drains a wide berth.

Benny kicked a bottle on the ground with the tip of his shoe. It spun around in the dirt several times, finally coming to a rest.

The bottleneck pointed under the overpass, to Eastside.

****

Benny drove slowly, cautiously. He stopped at every cross street, squinting his eyes as he gazed into the distance. He looked down every alley, cursing the muddy darkness that pooled in each narrow dead-end avenue. He watched as shadowy figures passed by fourth-story windows in brick warehouses that had been vacated decades ago; he peered into the windows of these buildings upon seeing the flickering orange and red of bonfires blazing somewhere deep within.

It was a big old town, and it was rotten at the core.

Once a thriving industrial complex, a center for steel mills and coal-driven textile factories, now the Eastside was a crumbling old slum. Cops steered clear of these blocks, and even pushers wouldn't dare tread here unarmed. Here dwelled only individuals that society had long ago forsaken.

Although Benny did not understand the connection yet, he knew that something linked the events taking place in Eastside with the murders. 9th Street Harry could probably explain it to him, but somehow Benny didn't expect to find him alive.

Benny's foot punched the brake.

He watched something race along the opposite sidewalk toward him. It ran several feet, then stopped, then darted off again. It was small and low to the ground. It looked too big to be a rat.

Suddenly, it burst out into the street. As it crossed a couple of feet in front of Benny's old Chrysler, it was bathed in the glare of his headlights.

As if caught unaware, it stopped, wheeled about, and faced him.

It was a hairless rodent with a long tail and big ears. Benny had never seen something quite so repulsive. Its fangs glistened in the headlight; its pale flesh twitched. Its tail whipped back and forth hypnotically.

It stood up straight as if it was trying to get a better look at Benny. Its front limbs dangled, its claws fidgeting.

Then it scurried off down a sewer drain.

Ten minutes later, Benny was struggling to free a manhole cover from its place. He stared down into the dark abyss of the city sewer system. With a strong flashlight in hand and his Ithica Roadblocker strapped to his back, Benny descended into the bowels of the inner city.

He cautiously worked his way down the cold, metal rungs of the ladder, occasionally shining his flashlight beneath him, trying to judge the distance to the tunnel floor. He heard a trickle of water flowing below, and the stench of the place stained his lungs.

Benny paused. He heard something moving directly beneath him. He fumbled for his flashlight, thumbed the toggle switch. A burst of light ignited the floor ten feet below. A pair of bright, red eyes glared back at him; then, whatever it was shot off into the shadows.

Benny crept slowly along the narrow path that ran beside the stream of stewing, swirling black sewage. Rats—things he could identify as rats—stared at him as he shuffled by. The air inside the tunnel was hot and thick, and the stench was enough to make Benny gag. It was not long, however, before he recognized a different scent masked by the sewage; it was an odor he had smelled many times before. He smelled death.

As he walked further, the smell of rotting corpses became so overpowering that Benny had to cover his mouth and nose with a handkerchief. His eyes watered. His mind reeled. How many bodies would he find down here?

Benny came out of the tunnel into a large, open chamber. He recognized it as an intersection where several smaller sewer lines merged into one enormous drainage pipe. Benny figured that the main line probably ran to the processing plant.

A few emergency lights in the distant corners of the room offered up some light, but vast stretches were flooded in darkness. Benny strained his eyes as he searched the shadows with his flashlight.

He saw the blue before anything else. The initial sight of it made him giddy, and he wobbled backward. It was a leg ... but there was more. Much more.

In one corner of the room was a mountain of corpses, stacked on high, alive with rats. Now that his light bathed the scene, he could hear their jagged teeth gnawing away at the flesh and muscle over the gentle rush of the sewage. He could hear millions of flies scatter upon sensing his presence. And what horrified him the most was that he could hear someone in the hideous mass moaning, someone that wasn't quite dead yet and knew precisely what was happening.

His gaze was frozen upon the sight. The hand holding the handkerchief slowly dropped from his mouth. He felt his knees weaken and knew that he was sinking toward the floor. Disgust mingled with awe. What lay before him made him want to run and scream, yet it begged him to stay and study it.

As he stared at the pile of carcasses, a dozen things he thought were rats stood up. They spotted him. He recognized the sudden anger in their eyes, knew that they considered him an unwelcome trespasser on their territory. With speed that took his breath away, and with an agility that made him gasp, the things abandoned their feast and took to the walls. They scurried up the sides of the chamber and across its ceiling as they made their way toward him.

Benny, now on his knees, wanted to retreat, wanted his fingers to find the security of the Roadblocker strapped to his back. He wanted to cry out and implore whatever gods existed to put an end to this nightmare. His body simply would not cooperate. He was completely paralyzed.

Fear bubbled up the back of his throat and spattered out across his lips.

The first of the things to reach him lunged from the ceiling and lit upon his shoulder. It grasped his flesh with its claws coiled its tail around his neck. Its hind legs slipped and razor-sharp claws tore through his shirt and shredded the skin of his chest.

When it began snapping at the back of his neck, biting away tiny chunks of flesh and muscle, Benny's paralysis subsided.

As he fought his way back to his feet, Benny dropped his flashlight. It cracked and its glass lens shattered when it hit the floor. Its light whimpered and flashed a few times before fading.

His hand clamped over the loose skin of the rodent-thing. His fingers wound around its bony frame. Its hide was cold and slimy. Benny grunted with pain as he wrenched the monster free and hurled its writhing body to the ground.

Before it could regain its balance and renew its attack, Benny's foot came down over its head and crushed its skull. Milky brown ooze seeped out over his shoe. He recoiled in sudden disgust, then kicked the thing out into the black pool of sewage.

As the air licked his numerous wounds, he hissed. He wondered how much of his flesh was caught beneath the thing's nails and between its sharp fangs. He let his hand cover the back of his neck where the rodent-had bitten him, and though he could feel the blood soaking his shirt and running down his back, he still was shocked by the sight of his palm dripping crimson.

And it was far from over.

The other rodent-things had stood by silently as their scout had tested Benny's strength. Now a second approached, followed quickly by another. Four more took a circuitous route that would allow them to come up behind him.

Benny wouldn't allow another to come close enough to bleed him. His Colt Diamondback felt good in his hand. He was no fool—he had learned how quick these things were. He waited until they were practically upon him, until he could smell the corpse-meat on their breaths.

He splattered one as it leapt toward him from the wall. Another, apparently frightened by the sight of its companion's quivering body, froze in its tracks. Benny picked it off cleanly, sending its body flailing into the shadows. The remainder were less eager to meet their deaths and scattered into the shadows.

Benny felt the thrill of a Neanderthal after the mastodon had been felled by his clumsy, blunt-tipped spears.

Now he turned, ready to flee—ready to find help to sort out this mess of bodies and uncanny flesh-eating rodents.

"I am afraid we cannot let you leave." The voice thundered down the sewage corridors and pricked Benny's flesh. "You will only bring others, others that would do far more damage than you have done this evening."

Benny turned back toward the chamber. Floating inches above the surface of the filthy water was a young man, naked except for the shadows that he wrapped about himself. Though his face was shrouded in the gloom, his eyes sparkled with an eerie radiance, and they glared across the distance and pierced Benny's soul. They immediately revealed a sense of familiarity and an unsettling feeling of antiquity.

"Who are you?" Benny asked.

"I am ekimmu—fourth generation. And these are my younger brothers..." His hands swept out from the cloak of darkness which clothed him, his upturned palms aglow with a strange and wondrous white light. From the shadows stepped the remaining rodent-things, clicking their nasty teeth and hissing at Benny. "We were thirteen strong until you came along."

Benny studied the man in the fresh light. His face was that of a classic Greek god: Smooth and taut flesh, with a strong square jaw and prominent eyebrows. His hair was coal-black, and confined in tiny tight curls. Still, it was his eyes that bore his whole character. In them, Benny could find traces of power and hunger. Benny's keen instants begged him to run, but at the same time assured him that nothing could save him now.

"What are you?" Benny rephrased his previous question since the answer had been beyond his comprehension.

"We are the shepherds of your civilization, sir." He smiled, revealing long and primal fangs. With a wave of his hand, he dispersed his kin who scurried back to the mound of rotting corpses. He then walked over the surface of the water toward Benny, pulling the cloak of shadows around his form as he did so. By the time he stood a few feet away, the intangible darkness had become a very tangible silky fabric that was draped over his shoulders. "Please excuse my attire—I have only recently passed into this body."

"You mean ... you were like them?" Benny looked over at the rodent-things, busily devouring the dead to quench their ravenous appetites. He was only now beginning to understand.

"Yes ... and soon, they too will form cocoons wherein they will undergo the transformation. This is simply one stage of their life cycle."

"Part of which," Benny mumbled to himself, "Is spent inside a living host ... which provides them the initial nourishment they require in their developmental stages." Benny's mind thought of maggots eating their way through an animal corpse.

"An interesting analogy," the man said. He had read Benny's thoughts, plucked the image straight out of his head. "And not altogether incorrect. Except it is not really the blood and flesh that we crave. We consume these only to reach the soul."

Benny shuddered. It was not the words that frightened him, but the casual way in which they were spoken. Something that conveyed their truth instantly.

"Why now? Why here?"

"We only spawn every thousand years. The last of our preceding generation was here when he realized he was dying. He impregnated thirteen people before he passed on." He looked toward the mound of corpses, smiling as his brothers grew stronger on the souls of the dead and dying. "Now we must continue the mission."

"Mission?"

"Yes. As I said before, we have served as shepherds to your society, guiding it toward its zenith. We have taken you from the savannas where your nomadic ancestors hunted game and brought you to the brink of space travel."

"Why?"

"We alone could never have achieved what you mortals have achieved. You have developed the technology and built the infrastructure required for interstellar space travel. Of course, it would have taken mankind another two hundred thousand years to forge the most rudimentary of civilizations had we not intervened." He shook his head upon recognizing the confusion in Benny's bewildered stare. "Don't you see—we are not of your world. We have been marooned here for a hundred thousand years. Each succeeding generation has driven your race toward supplying us with the equipment we require to return to our home world!"

Benny stared back down the long line of written history. He thought about how the human race has surged forward, racing toward some unknown objective. He saw then, in that moment, that progress did not come steadily like a flowing river. Instead, it seemed forced upon civilization in inconsistent spurts and was always linked with conflict. Inevitably, it appeared, the advancements that led to the development of space-faring technology seemed spurred on by war or rage or intolerance.

"And this is how you thank us for centuries of blind slavery?" Benny motioned toward the mound of putrefying corpses. He began to back away slowly, dragging his feet over the slippery floor. "You've plagued us for years, haven't you? You are the vampires ... the werewolves. You are the monsters in the forests and the dragons in the caves. Everything you have done has pushed us further toward achieving your goals." He stopped; his fingers reached for the Roadblocker strapped to his back. "How many wars did you start so that weapons technology could be advanced? Who do you count among your ancestors? Alexander the Great? Genghis Khan? Napoleon? Hitler?"

Benny brought forth his scattergun, resting its barrel in his left hand while the index finger of his right hand played over the trigger.

"You are no more murderous now than when we found you. You were nomadic butchers, brawling over parcels of ground and the rotting carcasses of beasts."

"How can you call us butchers..." Benny looked toward the corpses again, and a thought occurred to him.

"We have only done what was necessary to survive."

"Survival," muttered Benny. "That's all that's important isn't it?" Benny's finger shuddered and the Roadblocker growled and kicked at the same time. The vampiric entity lunged forward to avoid the shot, but found that he was not the intended target.

In a fraction of an instant, the thing understood what was happening. Even as the projectiles were racing toward the far end of the chamber, toward the fuse box that controlled the emergency lights, the thing acted to save its kind from extinction. Its speed was unearthly. It moved so fast that Benny could only see a dull black blur.

It still wasn't fast enough.

There was a tinny snap followed by a shower of sparks as the shot penetrated the fuse box. Flames issued forth almost immediately. Gently they lapped at the chamber wall, reaching for the ceiling.

"NO!" the alien shrieked, and his younger brothers looked up from their feast.

The lights went out, but the darkness was fleeting.

When the fiery fingers touched the invisible clouds of methane hovering in the sewer and the gases began to burn, Benny saw more colors than he ever knew existed. Then a blinding flash surged over him. It devoured everything in its path. It boiled the black and filthy water. It warped and cracked the pavement on the streets above. It blew manhole covers into the sky.

It ended the silent subjugation of mankind.

The End

The Canoe
by
Ruth A. Deming

Lake Galena was open for the season. Several people lined up to rent canoes and kayaks. The water smelled from fish. Canoes and kayaks were already floating along the smooth waters.

"Wanna go in one canoe?" asked the fellow behind me.

"Why not?" I said. "By the way, my name is Cindy."

"I'm Rob," he said.

After all, what could happen in a single canoe?

"I took time off work," he said. "I run a small print shop in Lansdale. My clients are faithful to me and don't use desktop publishing."

We each rowed, stroke by stroke.

"This is so delightful," I said, looking at the clouds. When my kids were young, we would make shapes from the clouds.

"A roly-poly clown!" I said, pointing to the sky.

"I love a woman with a good imagination," he said.

"I own an art gallery – *Peacocks* – in the resort town of New Hope. Ever hear of it?"

"Where Jessica Savitch drowned," he said.

"One and the same," I said.

He proposed that we try to drown ourselves in Lake Galena, that it was next to impossible.

"Rob! Are you frigging kidding me?"

At that, he dropped the paddle in the lake, stood up, and rocked the boat.

Sure enough, it tipped over.

He pushed me until I was underneath. My head was barely above the water. He swam over and pulled my head under the water.

We both were wearing orange life vests.

I swam over to him and grabbed his genitals and squeezed as hard as I could.

He let go of me and I swam quickly onto the lake itself and off toward the shore.

My screams were heard by several people who came to help me.

"That man tried to murder me," I said.

I only hoped the police would believe me.

The End

Memories of Evil Spirits by Matthew Wilson

There's a woman outside my window without a face
The knife clutched in her claws gleams in the moonlight
Sometimes I notice her out the corner of my eye whilst working
There's a woman outside my window without a face.

Rain from the thunderstorm runs down the flat flesh on her skull
The eyeless watching membrane devoid of emotion
She is never there when I call friends or police over

Her gentle falling feet leave no footprint in the promising dawn.

I have not heard her breathing disturb the scuttling spiders there
Being so careful as not to knock them from the glass
But still I feel her presence when I close the curtains
Jiggling the lock to see if I forgot to lock up before bed.

There's a woman outside my window without a face
Since my wife's passing, this thing has come from nowhere
Waiting with a moonlight gleaming knife aimed at me
Like an avenging spirit to kill my wife's killer.

Bead Trickling Laughter
by
S. M. Bidwell

The sealed plastic bag contained a comb, strands of hair ensnared, and a lipstick, color labeled as cinnamon. A purse held credit and debit cards scratched from overuse, a little cash, plus many out-of-date receipts for petrol, Cheryl one for always being on the road.

The woman on the other A broken chain in the coin compartment came from a trinket she loved and kept meaning to have repaired. The knowledge she now never would brought pain and emotions I held back as I examined her phone from which the police had retrieved my number. Last of the contents comprised two sets of door keys, and a small notebook or diary with a lock but no key. Along with a handbag, these items represented an inadequate snapshot of Cheryl's life.

side of the desk who handed over the paltry evidence of my adopted sister's existence checked the list twice, giving me a polite but insincere apology. "I'm afraid this is everything. Sorry. If a key isn't on the list, there wasn't one." She stared at me with one raised eyebrow as though I sounded accusing. The notion irritated me though I didn't argue, having suffered enough.

During the journey home in the driving rain, I went over the details of Cheryl's demise as imparted to me. Strangers found her lying on the outside stairs with her head pointed downward, her face to the side with an expression described as terror. The conjecture alleged she hurried from the house on Church Hill, tripped, and fell. The autopsy confirmed the blow against concrete steps cracked her skull. Her expression they took for one of shock when she failed to stop herself from falling. The authorities as good as declared accidental death before someone finished stitching her back together.

The handbag now occupying the passenger seat, police found sprawled a few steps further down, the bag having tumbled. I glanced at the pink leather now, wishing an inanimate object could tell me what I needed to know. I directed my attention back to the road aware I wished for the impossible. The headlights from another car flashed strobe-like through the darkness, blinding. As my vision cleared, so did my mind.

Perhaps the answers would come from the notepad contained therein. Though minus the key, a screwdriver and hammer would soon break the lock open.

****

The police not bothering to read the notebook might have seemed a little strange but not in the small secluded coastal town of Hawnporth. There folks, including the fuzz, did things their own way, and in a clear-cut case of accidental loss of life, everyone considered the least they did was sufficient. When I inquired, I learned no one so much as cared to search the house. What was the point when Cheryl passed away outside?

My pressing question concerning Cheryl's death was not how she died, though I wanted to understand that too. I longed to know what she was doing at the house. The moment we were both old enough, we seized the opportunity to get away, vowing never to return.

Taking in the ancient facade now, I questioned how I survived as a child entombed in its dark corridors and musty rooms. Church Hill got its name because if anyone cared to huff and puff to the top of the hill, a church, indeed, existed. In ruins now, the remains served as a token attraction or a place for teens to make out. A few houses stood spaced at a considerable distance down the hill but at too awkward an elevation to be desirable, especially not for the unlikely residents of Hawnporth.

Aunt Margaret was one of a few locals not to pass on or to swallow her losses relocating down in the village. Then a year ago, even Margaret went off to shoot the breeze with the Grim Reaper. Some people said she won; others claimed she lost. Neither Cheryl nor I had the nerve to seek the truth.

Carol Anne, you stand in the corner until I say you can move….

I jumped, feeling foolish, the internal dialogue the ghost of my past. If impressions were anything to go by, Cheryl was right and I was wrong in our bet as to whether Margaret remained alive, but there's a reason for saying appearances can be deceptive.

****

Aunt Margaret took me in when my parents died in a car accident. At the time, she also acted as a guardian for Cheryl by a court decision when authorities discovered the infant alone in a locked house. This occurred after Cheryl's mother, a distant relative of Margaret's, was arrested for drunk driving. Though the mother didn't run, acted calm, and stopped the car, she did nothing to enamor the law by opening the door and puking all over a police officer's shoes. The condition of the house and the number of empty booze bottles left the authorities no choice but to seek alternative accommodation for the child. A strict mandate for the woman commanded she not get Cheryl back until she made it through rehab. Cheryl never saw her mother again and attempts to locate her father failed, so they entrusted her to Margaret.

By the time my parents met their disastrous end, Cheryl's mother had disappeared into the darkness of drug abuse. Margaret followed through, doing what was necessary to prove herself a more than adequate substitute. Not that I imagined anyone being overly picky, not back when we were growing up, and this was Hawnporth where people did things their own way. The temporary situation became permanent. Cheryl and I of similar age and best friends almost right away, Margaret pressed the reason of not wishing to break up our happy family. Though logical, the process moved so fast simply because Margaret was rich enough to care for herself and two children without working. In reality, I'm sure, the way Margaret presented herself and her ability to grease wheels, palms, and for all I knew lightning itself, had a lot to do with the outcome. In this community, people seized easy opportunities.

She refused payment, so they placed the monthly subsidy for our guardianship in a fund for when we came of age. I'm glad because that money helped us to get away, but that was much later.

So began my strange life at Number 9 Church Hill, the one but last residence on a steep ascent. Coming home from school on a hot day was a slog, yet Cheryl and I were grateful we took so long to reach the top.

Home is where the heart is, they say.

I won't pretend I had a nightmare upbringing in this three-story Victorian with its bay windows and dusty loft, but it was a peculiar time. Margaret's penchant for never throwing anything out and collecting paraphernalia others binned made the house into a museum. The back garden and the surrounding land became a vicious scrapyard.

Margaret would disappear for hours, leaving Cheryl and me to entertain and rear ourselves in this mausoleum. Her reappearances were often sudden enough to spook the life out of a person, materializing ghostlike or as a distorted shadow in my or Cheryl's peripheral vision. After a time, I developed the ability to sense her presence. Though this awareness — the knowledge she hid somewhere, watching, silent, secret — scared me, I learned to hide my fear and my understanding. The insight was my advantage, not hers, and she would not be pleased with the discovery. My first reactions I pretended happened because I spotted her by accident; but for ages, she remained suspicious. Once I could sense her, she watched me, waiting for a sign I hid my awareness. I deliberately messed up a few times until she dismissed her misgivings. Better a punishment than more surveillance. Over time, our lives fitted a pattern, becoming what accounted for normal in our house, but the question remained: why did Margaret spy on us? Did she intend to catch us in some kind of wrongdoing?

Margaret was a quiet woman. Whenever she spoke, she was giving one of us an order or a scolding. Often her reprimands presented themselves in a fit of temper, sometimes worse, with a sweet smile and a nasty glint in her eyes. I preferred her fury. The woman's displeasure was far more sinister when she sounded almost kind. The twinkle in her gaze and her chuckle haunted me long after I left. As I aged, other questions bothered me. Having less than a liking for us, why did Margaret want to take on the care of two young girls she didn't love?

The kindness of her heart?

No.

A sense of duty?

Maybe, but although Cheryl's mother and Margaret were distantly related, the title of Aunt struck me as having no actual meaning of kinship. If she took Cheryl in because of being related to her, why include me? As Cheryl's companion? Cheryl and I often puzzled over the same thing.

Striding across the threshold now I took a step back through time, the tinkle of Cheryl's laughter pealing out, fading fast, muffled by mildewed walls. Our feet beat a path from room to room, up the stairs, down, booming against bare boards whenever Margaret vanished. We only felt free during her absences. When she occupied the house, we remained quiet.

The furniture still stood in all the positions I recollected. Everything lackluster in dull shades, blended into one murky hue, almost as though the sun bleached everything, though far from true. Margaret favored thick heavy drapes and intricate lace curtains capable of trapping the dust and flies. Still, a modicum of light sneaked by. She never once took the draperies down to have them cleaned. If able, I'm sure she would have preferred to paint the windows black same as I was about to do now.

I chose the lounge. Only two doors led inside, and the space contained the largest window. I threw back the nets, almost choking on the disturbed dust, blinded by the sheer magnitude of motes the meager sunlight pinpointed floating. Next, I pushed a few pieces of furniture to one side of the room. Nothing too obvious, or too heavy — I tried to make no noise — but moved anything small or in an awkward position, items inclined to trip me or hinder movement. In the lower part of the house, I went about opening doors, locking or blocking others. I chose a trail and left no options open. Dim illumination filtering through drab textiles brought on a twilight not good enough for my purpose.

From the basement door I worked back, retracing my steps, painting all the windows black. I slapped paint anywhere snatches of light showed through, so no rips in the fabric, or when covers crumbled from mold altogether, could reveal the outside world. Inside the house, I changed the time to midnight.

The basement door creaked while I slogged, one room away from my destination. So I steadied my breath, fought to control my galloping heart rate, and concentrated on the task. The last thing I did was to paint the huge window in what Margaret always called the drawing room. I turned my back on the glass, sat down on the sofa, closed my eyes in the darkness, and prepared to wait.

In the inky gloom of my making, I reached out to either side and patted my limited arsenal. To my left lay Cheryl's diary with a torch. To my right, I placed a small horde of cricket balls.

Mine was a pathetic idea… too simple to work, but the plan was my only scheme.

People say when a person loses one of their senses, the others compensate. A soft shuffle and a scrape sounded so thunderous in the otherwise silent house; I swore she was already in the room with me. My imagination lied, but I opened my eyes, scaring myself as the inability to see increased my panic. Instinct compelled me to search, to spot what was coming. I forced my eyes shut though doing so made no difference. I stayed still by sheer will, focusing on the noises as they grew. My nape crawled, hair rising, fright breathing over my scalp and whispering to my nerves as the haunting presence entered. Still, I sat, not moving … until she clasped my ankle.

****

The recollection of the words written in Cheryl's diary froze me, but to remain immobile would be a literal death. Still, I struggled to break my paralysis until I became convinced I never would. Her laughing saved me. Bead trickling laughter as Cheryl referred to it… like a broken necklace and the beads scattering across the floor. Don't ask me why she described it so but the description fitted. The sound of beads rolling came back as chuckling rumbled out, making me grip my torch. I flicked on the light before opening my eyes, for the sudden brightness would blind me the same way it did Margaret.

I squinted, adjusting faster, in part because I understood what was coming, in part because of the sight of the creature before me.

Margaret. More used to the dark all these years, for her, the light proved far more disturbing.

Aunt Margaret, or what remained of her, lay motionless, eyes squeezed tight, caught trying to take of my leg a bite. She closed her mouth with a snap, turning her head, blinking, peering through the sudden glare, giving me a glimpse of strange opaque white and yellow eyes.

Her topknot tumbled half-undone and her fading yellow hair shared the same blend of eye color, blonde and white. Her old-fashioned style and tattered dress, dull with a floral pattern made me think of her as quaint, a perverse old-world charm hanging about her as though she were an ancient exhibit. I guess it's what a living death does to a person.

She, like the house, was covered in dust. Her body ended at the waist, which explained the sliding sound — Margaret dragging her remains around. Entrails of material and putrefied flesh trailed along the floor in her wake, a sight for which I hadn't prepared, yet… she was pitiful. Strange, the visage which should fill me with dread — should cause me to flee, perhaps die, petrified as Cheryl had — failed to scare me. True, nosing into Cheryl's diary forewarned me, but my lack of reaction was down to more than that.

Curiosity or anxiety won out — Cheryl checking on Aunt Margaret's disappearance from society, from the village, no one having seen her in months. No one bothered to undertake more than a cursory investigation of the house. What did they care? An eccentric old lady kept to herself or might have died. No one worried in Hawnporth.

I tried to imagine Cheryl as she penned the details. Trapped here for hours in the kitchen, escaping through the window too considerable a peril owing to the sharp accumulated debris. I would have tried, but Cheryl … always a clumsy girl, had tripped and fallen down the outside stairs anyway and done what Margaret failed to do, killing herself. The pain of never again being able to tease Cheryl for her propensity to self-injury came home. Cheryl died here, having written all this down … hoping someone might find her notes should she never leave.

Entrapped and all the while the skeletal frame of Aunt Margaret rattled the doorknob, called out to her, teased and tormented, perhaps tried to reassure with empty words of love. Easier to visualize this dead woman enjoying Cheryl's ordeal.

Ironic … my sister's last plan to abscond, to elude Margaret, led to Cheryl's dying. Whatever the circumstances, Aunt Margaret was responsible.

I laughed, making the corpse jerk back, stupefied, prompting me to chuckle more.

"Was it worth it, Margaret? Selling your soul for this pitiful existence?"

Words emerged almost unintelligible — unsurprising, considering the snake of a tongue I glimpsed flicking between her ivory teeth — but I understood her.

"Your faulttssss," she hissed. "Yours and Chhhhheryl's. Meant tttttoooo be here. Meanttttt ttttooo be my sssssssssacrificcccces."

Ah… Whatever black magic Margaret conjured, she had intended Cheryl and I be integral.

"Tough break," I told her, and stood, clasping a cricket ball. A shake of my leg disengaged her grip, and though she snarled, I still felt no fear of her.

A demented leer spread over her face before she snapped at me, but I wasted no more time, stepped aside, spun and threw the ball. My accuracy had improved with practice, but I was still surprised when I shattered a whole pane of glass. Without a pause I picked up another missile, aimed, and lobbed it at another section of the window. Sunlight penetrated the room, chasing Margaret's expression of surprise and horror, as she jerked back to escape a sunbeam.

I took up a third ball and tossed it up and down in my hand. "One other thing. It's not night time, you daft old bat."

She pulled away, hindered by my stepping on her entrails, screaming at me, coming for me, hands curling into claws. I pitched. Glass exploded. Light flooded the room. Struck.

I glanced in time to observe Margaret's desiccated skin blister and crack, though I backed up as she erupted into dust.

I'd learned much from Cheryl's words. Whatever kind of creature Aunt Margaret became, she didn't like the light. The sun made her flesh steam. No matter what bargain she made with a demon, it did not amaze me a few restricting rules applied to a living dead woman ever moving about in the daytime.

I went back through the house, flinging open doors and curtains, breaking windows where they wouldn't budge, to let the light in and fresh air. This time I made my way beyond the basement door into the kitchen where I discovered what happened to the rest of Margaret. The old heavy pine dresser lay on the floor and trapped Margaret from the waist down. Must have taken the strength of terror to push the weight over, the sad truth being Cheryl had no reason to give in to blind panic, killing herself by accident. Margaret, unable to release herself any other way had literally torn her body in two, to be free. The legs still kicked, feebly. A simple solution was to open the curtains and let the sun take care of everything.

A cleaning crew is due to stop by soon. I'm Margaret's only kin, and in Hawnporth no one will question me moving back into the house. The building needs work, but I'm sure I'll enjoy the project, and, in time, I plan to check out Margaret's extensive library. Somewhere in those pages I'm sure to find a whole other level of existence.

The End

Second Thoughts
by
Rod Marsden

In the year 2095, Rose had flown past Darwin with its picturesque park land and was heading out to sea. She would fly past Port Moresby in Papua, New Guinea with its modern housing and airport and also East Timor with its bright Roman Catholic churches.

This was her first bombing run, and her target was Jakarta in Indonesia. She expected to be intercepted by Indonesian fighters as she approached Bali, and she wasn't disappointed. She had, however, speed and maneuverability on them, and they were quickly shot down.

To keep from feeling negative, she thought of what she was doing as a computer game. She had to win, of course, to stay alive. *Two blips on my console, and now they're gone. Yay me!*

Other Australian fighter bombers were targeting different parts of Indonesia though no one had Bali in their sights. Neither the Australian nor the American government wanted to nuke that island. For a century, it had been a friendly spot for Westerners. Jakarta, however, had become a definite hostile.

For decades, the Australian government had thrown billions at the Indonesian elite to no noticeable avail. Their government had continued to treat Australia and Australians with contempt. Something had to give and, when the religious wars began, that was it. After Sydney was attacked, the USA gave the Australian government the okay to retaliate.

Coming into the release range for her nukes, Rose saw small, decrepit boats on the harbor and, further in, hovels surrounded by glistening skyscrapers. She couldn't help but think that those who deserved to perish were probably in the thousands, and she was going to eliminate millions. It simply wasn't fair.

She hesitated over the release button and had to circle around for a second try. While she was doing that, an Indonesian jet fighter got on her tail. She flew up and around to be where she could nail the creep. When she blew apart the miscreant's canopy with her machine guns, she was close enough to see the expression of horror on her adversary's face. It was there for only a second, then he was gone, fallen from the sky. So much for imagining this was only a computer game.

Rose did not shy away the second time. The button pressed, she peeled off in the direction of home. A great white light blinded her for a minute, and she knew it was over for the thousand or so culprits and the millions of innocents. She thought she felt a demonic presence for a moment but put that down to her imagination.

She hoped she would never be called upon to do this to any other city; but there was a war on and she was a fighter bomber pilot.

The End

Journey into Night by Marc Shapiro

Walking through thousands of unchartered worlds
I am blinded
But I can see
The living dead rise
To point my way

Onward to where
To the endless trek
Oblivion says go
Onward
To my just rewards

Evening Flea Market
by
Trisha Ridinger McKee

Ethel tapped her hair with the palm of her hand to ensure it was crunchy enough to stay in place. Knowing this night was vital, she added an extra stream of hairspray just to be sure. And then she clipped the large fake daisy to the side of her head, flinching as her hair flattened in that spot.

For the hundredth time that night, she wished the old wives' tales were true. She wished she did not have to go through this tedious, nerve-wracking ritual every single time. Women did not enjoy spending hours getting ready, and the older one got, the longer it took to look halfway as enticing as when one was younger.

Finally, her faded yellow hair was properly poofed and sprayed, the flower in place, appearing as if it were merely a fun afterthought and not a pain in the ass that it was. But the flower was her signature look. Whimsical. Flirty. Young at heart.

Ethel did not need to add any type of foundation to her skin. As wrinkled as it was, her complexion was an even shade, pale but even. She did add some rouge to her cheeks, cursing the feel of her saggy, thin skin, like tissue paper.

The last step of this long, ridiculous ritual was the lipstick. Her signature color - red. A deep red. She dipped her finger into the jar, noting that her unique homemade blend was low. This would be the last application until she could get more to mix up. Jutting her chin forward, she stared into the mirror and rubbed her stained finger across her chapped, thin lips.

"Okay, old girl. Showtime." The words made her smile, showcasing those painted lips. Years ago … hell, a lifetime ago, she had been in a few Broadway shows and had had a few bit parts in movies. She'd had a totally different life living among the rich and the beautiful. She had known and been known. It was a time that she learned to use her feminine powers to get what she wanted, a skill she still used today. Because age meant nothing when you knew how to treat a guy just right, how to wink at the right moment with enough subtlety to not be garish. How to tilt your head back and laugh lightly, lyrically. Age did not matter when a woman knew how to lift her eyes with her head lowered and smile just enough. Just enough so that the guy would grin stupidly at the attention.

Men were simply children that craved attention. Show the guy just what he wanted, give him that attention to make him feel desired and masculine, to make him feel needed … and he would give up the world for you. At least for a few moments.

Sure, being a semi-starlet had taught her a lot of tricks. Being a woman gave her power. Back in her day, they did not need to protest or scream about equal pay. She had her bills paid and food in the cupboards. She had precious gems dripping from her ears and neck, weighing down her fingers. Back in those early days, being an actress paid little. But being wooed by men gave her everything she could want or need. A job? Her job was seducing without being obvious. To hook a man and make him think he was doing the chasing. It was a learned skill. No. It was a talent.

With a wistful sigh, she gave herself one more study in the mirror before giving a short nod and leaving.

The summer evening was comfortable; the sun's exit eliminated the stifling heat. Ethel was blanketed in warmth as she strolled to her car. She almost hated to leave her home, to leave this property. She would much rather sit outside and stare at the stars. But she was getting restless, itchy, and that ache was growing from the middle of her chest outward, like arms stretching out in all directions to grab and twist and destroy. She had to focus and forge ahead, had to allow the intensity of that ache to drive her.

The flea market was still empty as she made her way to her booth. Bare light bulbs swung overhead, casting a golden light that barely broke through the shadows. It was lighting that she knew made her look a little less pale, a little less old. The place smelled musty, and she could hear the clanging of dishes and cups in the cafe one room over. That was what brought the bulk of the business in the evenings. Truck drivers stopped for coffee at that all-night diner, and they usually ended up moseying down the aisles of the flea market afterward.

The flea market was located in the middle of nowhere, but on Saturday and Sunday mornings, it still drew a crowd, with young couples looking for a good deal, families wanting to get out of the house, and elderly couples meeting friends and searching for a knick-knack to add to their collections.

On Friday and Saturday evenings, the flea market and the cafe were open, but the crowd was thinner, more random. A lot of truck drivers, some teenagers, and the young couples could be seen wandering around, searching for the next great item. The aisles were quieter, dimmer, and only half the booths were open. Most vendors only wanted the prime busy time and didn't want to waste precious evening time in a dingy building with only half the crowd.

"Hey, well lookie there. Ethel!"

Ethel glanced up, smiling vaguely at the pot-bellied, balding man standing in front of her booth before she continued removing the tarp from her tables. "Hi, Ben."

He moved forward to help, bouncing animatedly. "Oh, you should have been here this morning, Ethel! Biggest crowd yet. I sold my log planter. Been trying to move that for months!"

"Really? Oh, my. For daisy."

"Yes! And a few people asked about your purses. Listen, I don't understand why you don't come in earlier. You could sell so much more."

"I've already told you. I tend to my garden during the day. I don't want to waste sunshine in here."

He widened his eyes and lifted a shoulder. "Well, you don't know what you're missing out on."

It was the same conversation every Saturday night. And when he lingered at her booth, even as a few kids snooped around his booth, she prepared herself.

"How about we go grab some coffee afterward?"

"No, Ben."

"Why don't you ever want to get a coffee? You seein' someone, you sly girl?"

She gave him a forced smile and lifted her eyebrows. "I am. I tell you this every week."

"I've never seen him."

She leaned sideways and called out over his shoulder, "Those are breakable! Please don't touch unless you're buying!" She turned her attention back to Ben, nodding toward his booth. "You'd better get back to work before they clear you out." She knew Ben's breaking point was teenagers, and she heaved a sigh of relief when he did a double-take and then stomped over to his booth, his steps heavy and arms pumping.

Ethel worked at organizing her items, purses spread out on one side table, books in a few piles in the corner, candles and incense on the other side, and jewelry in the front. She had some knick-knacks that she put on the back table. The flea market was saturated with knick-knacks, but she was confident she had the best. No stains or chips. They were like new. She had cardinals and clowns, dogs of almost every breed, and small, fake flowers in tiny vases. She had a vast assortment, and she knew Ben was right. If she could come in the mornings and early afternoons, she would make a killing. She giggled at that choice of words.

But her purpose had little to do with sales and everything to do with making a living ... literally.

Just as she got everything set up, people started to mill in, casually strolling, moving their heads from one side to another, gawking at the tables. Sometimes she felt irritation pinch up her spine as she watched these strangers stare down her items as if judging. But she pasted on that bright smile and widened her eyes to give that vapid look.

"Jewelry, huh?"

Ethel spun around and smiled up at a tall older gentleman wearing suspenders and a t-shirt full of holes, his pants coated with oil and food stains. He looked slightly out of place. But just slightly. Truck driver. "Yes, sir, jewelry. Can I show you some pieces? Big handsome fella like you has to have a sweetheart tucked away just waiting for that special gift."

"Me? Naw. I'm all kinds of single. Don't need the headache." He moved his hand out of view, but she had already seen that gold circle highlighting his lies.

It was actually better that he was married. The married ones tended to keep any indiscretions quiet. They were less likely to brag to their friends of any impending plans, any details. Sure, the married ones might have someone looking for them eventually, but truck drivers were known for disappearing. Long drives, longer sleeps, unanswered calls, it was all part of the lifestyle.

She noticed he was still talking, although she could recite the words by heart. Men tended to stick to the same script. "But I might be able to tolerate the headache if it were for someone as pretty as you. I like that there flower in your hair."

"Why, thank you!" She cast her gaze down with a soft smile, and her hand floated to the flower, her fingertips grazing it as if she had forgotten it was there. She focused on a woman that was browsing the books. "I'd better get back to selling. If you decide to pick up any jewelry, stop back."

Ethel made a point to not watch him walk away, to curb the excitement because she knew she had an audience. Ben would be watching, and that Zelda a few booths over always had to be in her business. Ethel knew Zelda was not even her real name. She had to make up some fancy name because the rest of her was so dull.

As if reading her thoughts, Zelda waved her hand back and forth. "Yoo-hoo, Ethel!"

She forced the obligatory smile, throwing her hand up in a weak greeting. "Zelda."

She stifled a groan as Zelda lurched forward and marched the short distance between them. Her puffy face was stained red with the effort of the extra steps, and her eyes looked nondescript and glossy. Ethel always believed the most beautiful thing about a woman should be her eyes, and she trusted no female that had average eyes.

"Who was that guy you were talking to?"

Keeping her tone even, she asked, "What guy?" She turned to the woman browsing. "I have a sale going on. Three for five dollars. That includes hardbacks."

Zelda's dirty hair flopped around as she shook her head in exasperation. "That man you were just talking to."

"The customer? I don't know his name or anything, Zelda."

"Hmm. You looked cozy."

"Cozy? Like cozy as in comfortable? As comfortable as you are in those orange pants?"

"They're pink. I'm just saying ... you get awfully chummy with a lot of men."

Ethel smiled brightly at the customer as she brought over several books. She took her time bagging them up and taking the woman's money, watched her walk away before taking a deep breath and turning back to Zelda, her smile never wavering. "How's Roland?"

"Huh?" But there was that panic on the surface giving her away.

"How is he? Last time I saw him, he was coming out of the pantry closet with ... well, with you. Looking all disheveled and wide-eyed." She gave a light laugh. "I guess working in the cafe does that to a person." She winked.

Zelda's face turned such a dark red it would have been comical had Ethel not been so envious. To be allowed to lose one's emotions in that way, to express rage with a quivering voice and bold threats ... Ethel wished for that so many times. She would have loved to tell Zelda to take her frumpy frame and go home to her long-suffering husband. But she could not afford to call that kind of attention to herself. So she had to be content to drive weak-willed women like Zelda to the edge.

"You listen here, you ridiculous old biddy! I was not coming out of that room with him like that! I was looking to see if he had any fresh coleslaw in the back."

Ethel knew she had to diffuse the situation as people were turning to stare. "Okay, I never meant to insinuate anything. For daisy. What I intended to say was that he sure looked sweet on you. That's when you had your hair curled, remember? You drove the men crazy that weekend."

Zelda abruptly shut her mouth and drew back, as if slapped. Then she sputtered out thanks before scurrying back to her booth. But Ethel caught her fluffing that brownish-gray hair and knew she had succeeded in alleviating any agitation.

For the next hour, Ethel focused on customers trickling through the aisles. She sold a few more books and a purse. It was true that there was much more business in the early part of the day, but Ethel was satisfied with the sales she made in the evenings. It was enough. And it ultimately served a more important purpose.

There were fewer booths open than usual. Doug, the young man at the end of the aisle with model trains and cars, was absent. He was sporadic with his evening presence, and Ethel, for one, was relieved he was not there. He made her nervous. Several times she had glanced down the aisle to see him talking to himself. If he caught her looking, he would pretend to be singing, but she knew there was something not quite right there.

On the other end of the aisle, JoJo sold meats and soups. She would come in if the morning had been particularly busy and customers were returning. But she was not there; the corner was dark except for the flickering lights of the counter displays.

There was Mike two booths down. He had DVDs, CDs, and records. He was middle-aged, always snarling, never speaking. He would nod briskly if she greeted him, and then he would busy himself with arranging the merchandise, his underbite exaggerated as he nervously worked his jaw.

So there were fewer booths, but that meant that the customers would seek out the open businesses. People could say they came to simply browse, but they almost always came with the intention of buying something, anything. People loved junk. If they left without a bag in their hands, they felt empty.

Snippets of conversations floated from the aisles. She snapped back to the present to realize the truck driver was again in front of her.

"You sure are busy tonight."

She smiled, patting her hair. "Yes. Seems like a good night."

"So listen ... my name's Pete."

The way his mouth slowed down over the name, his tongue tripping, it was obviously a fake name. But she smiled. "I'm Ethel."

"Ethel. Mighty pretty name. Any chance you're single?"

This was so much more than a game. This was more than testing out flirting styles. Although Ethel had a lot of practice in this ritual, she still had to focus and be careful with every word, every movement. She had to get this right. There was too much on the line, and that ache in her chest was intensifying.

So yes, there was more to worry about than just hooking the guy. She had to ensure that their conversation looked like a business interaction to anyone watching, that he was a customer interested in something at her table. So as they spoke, she would lift up an item and show him, as if it were being discussed. She would nod and look away, rearranging the knick-knacks and glancing behind her as if to check the clock on the wall. Pure disinterest at its finest.

But then she would lean in close and answer in a soft purr with a slight smile. She knew it was puzzling for Pete, but he was transfixed, the confusion titillating. To him, this was a game, and when he walked away, his smile told a different story than what he displayed to those around them. Just as Ethel had intended.

She glanced over at Zelda and saw that her husband was there, so she caught Zelda's eye and waved, noting with a spark of joy that her face reddened and gaze shifted uneasily toward the clueless man in front of her. It just happened to be perfect timing as Roland strolled into sight. He barely glanced Zelda's way, but that did not stop her flush from darkening. Ethel guessed that Roland had appreciated the quickie from a willing participant but had no desire or need to push for anything more. He barely acknowledged either woman as he loped to the end of the aisle and scoured the display cases of meats. He scribbled something down and then dug through the case, and Ethel knew he was short on something at the cafe, and he and JoJo often exchanged goods and made deals. As he strolled back through the aisle, Ethel held in a giggle, seeing Zelda whisper frantically to her husband, probably attempting to get him to leave, thinking there might be a scene. She probably feared her secret would be revealed in a dramatic fashion, making her the scandal of the flea market.

But Roland merely glanced over at Ethel and gave her a slow wink, then whistled as he lumbered out of sight. She had always found him attractive for an older man with his full head of white hair and bright blue eyes, broad shoulders. But her rule was no local men, no getting involved. It was another thing she envied of Zelda, and perhaps that was where part of the teasing came from.

As the evening wore on, there were fewer couples and more teenagers, fewer families, and more truck drivers. And out came those women. The ones seeking the comfort and money of a man traveling through town. The ones with the gaunt faces and short skirts, always carrying the same expression of defeat and numbness.

They usually hung out in the parking lot, but some tried to slide inside, seeking shelter as they gave their spiel of forced smiles and throaty suggestions. Usually Carl, the maintenance manager of the building, kicked them out, or Roland shooed them away from the cafe.

They tended to be younger and more forward than Ethel, so they posed a bit of a problem. But they also presented a risk of getting arrested. Not to mention that while some of these men were willing to pay for sex, some weren't. There were still guys out there seeking just a taste of romance in the form of sincere flirting and general attraction.

A few of these women wandered the aisles; the sashaying of their hips contradicted the blank expressions aging their faces. Their painted lips curved up, but their eyes were dead. And with a jolt, Ethel realized she was similar to these women … more similar than she was comfortable with.

One of these women straightened and said out loud, "Cops." She turned, as if seeking reassurance or a partner, but seeing none, she rushed down the aisle and to the right, toward the exit.

Ethel saw the two cops clustered at the end of her aisle, speaking to Tanya, the young blond who sold facial creams and makeup that seemed like a good deal until you looked too closely at the expiration date.

Fighting to keep only curiosity showing on her face, Ethel watched the two uniformed men hold up a picture as Tanya squinted and then shrugged. She looked bored as the cops stayed a few minutes longer, no doubt lingering for a better look at her full cleavage.

"Wonder what this is about?"

She glanced up to see Ben. "Not sure."

Ben remained at her side as the cops made their way to her booth. "Good evening, folks. Don't want to keep you. Just need to know if you remember seeing this gentleman at all." The taller and thicker of the men held up a picture of a middle-aged man in a ball cap, sticking his head out the driver side window of a truck grinning as if he owned the world.

And Ethel had to be conscious again of her expression and not smile. Because she, of course, remembered him. One of the younger ones she had snagged. Confident little ass as he had strutted around the flea market, pointing to her and asking when she wanted to experience true paradise. She would have gagged had that ache not been consuming her. And had he not been young and handsome under the whiskers and grime and extra thirty pounds.

That was the last time she had soothed the ache.

Pulling at her stained lip, she shook her head. "I'm not sure, officer. We get so many people..."

"Of course. This would have been around four, five weeks ago. He had told his boss he was stopping here to grab some coffee, a bite to eat. Last anyone heard from him. His truck was found about thirty miles west of here. No sign of him."

Ben tilted his head, his finger poised mid-air. "Oh yeah! I do remember him. He was..." He stopped, throwing a glance Ethel's way before continuing, "He was in the cafe, and I think he might have walked around a little. I remember him because he was mouthy. Told me my prices were too high. But that's all I remember. I didn't see him leave with anyone."

"Okay. Thank you."

"Wait," Ben's hand shook as he held it up, palm out like one of those crossing guards trying to stop traffic. "This is like the third one in the area this year."

Fourth, Ethel corrected silently.

"Should we be worried?"

The shorter cop stood with his legs apart, his hands resting on his hips as if applying for superhero. "No. We don't think there's any reason to worry. There's a lot of woods. We think these guys just park and then go exploring. Get lost. But to be safe, try not to walk out at night alone." They left and walked to Zelda's booth, holding up the picture as if they had any interest in solving the case.

Ethel was still tugging at her dried, cracked lip when Ben asked, "That guy - you don't remember him?"

"No," she lied. "Should I?"

"He kept bugging you that night. Went to your booth like five different times. You looked irritated, and I almost went over to shoo him away for you."

"Never necessary," she assured him calmly. "I can take care of myself."

He stared at her, his hand subconsciously rubbing that over-inflated belly before he gave a short nod and walked back to his booth, dejected. He was anxious to play the hero in her life, and that almost made her laugh. She had lived a long life, experiencing true heroes, unexpected heroes, reluctant heroes … Ben was no hero, even though he did stop himself from telling the cops about the guy hanging all over Ethel. It saved her the inconvenience of pretending to forget and then recount some phony vague conversation that consisted of haggling over knick-knacks.

The cops in this area did not want the responsibility of solving a missing person case, much less a murder. To them, this was just a trucker passing through, getting lost in the woods when he walked too far to take a piss. The massive amounts of paperwork, if there were more to this, stopped them from trying too hard.

Ethel had been doing this long enough to be confident, to predict what would happen next. The only thing that made her a little panicky and fidgety was that damn growing ache that seemed to take over her thoughts and emotions as the night wore on. It was all she could do not to stare toward the entrance, waiting…

"Hello again. You're still here."

She glanced up, trying to control her smile. "Of course. Where else would I be?"

Pete leaned in with a smirk that prodded the sudden urge to smash her knuckles into his fleshy cheek. "I was hoping you'd be leaving with me."

"I'm here a couple more hours. But…"

"Should I come back?"

She pretended to think it over, although she knew just what was going to come out of her mouth. "What direction are you heading? Perhaps I can just meet you?"

Later that night, as she walked out of the building, some extra cash in her pocket, she tried to act tired, tried to avoid the goodbyes and plans to perhaps meet up during the week. A group of teenagers stood at the corner and sneered at her, calling out names and laughing. And she remembered several years back, in another place, with another group of teens, she had lost herself. She had dropped that shield she had to continually have up. She had revealed her true self with little more effort than to stop trying to be normal. And those kids had run off screaming. It was a satisfying moment until she realized she would have to start over. Another place. Another name.

"You kids shut up!" Ben barked, waving his hands at them as if they were merely mosquitoes to be brushed off. They laughed and called him a few choice words, but his attention was already on Ethel. "You goin' home, Ethel? Don't have time for a coffee?"

"Oh, I'm tired, Ben. It's late. I'll see you next week."

She got in her car and waited for him to leave. Last year, she had been followed halfway to her destination by that tiny guy with glasses, Leroy. He had had the booth two aisles over selling canned goods and had developed a crush. Fortunately, he sucked at being discreet, and she noticed his car before disaster had to happen. So now she was vigilant in watching, being aware. She knew she could not stay at this place forever … but she wanted to stay at least a bit longer. The setup, the location, the evening flea market … it was just convenient.

Pete was waiting right at the spot she had told him about. That hidden path invisible from the main road, barely wide enough for his large truck, and the forest swallowed it up, leaving no hint of its presence. Glints of moonlight streaked through the branches overhead giving them just enough light.

Sometimes Ethel wasted no time. But tonight … tonight she thought of Roland and that slow stroll of his, that sexy wink, and she indulged in sex, closing her eyes and trying to ignore this guy's sour breath and rolls of stomach smacking against her as his energy drained quickly.

Then there was no more postponing. That ache was crippling. Her lips had split open from the dryness. She needed to feed.

Ethel was not new to this. She had friends like herself, had exchanged stories. She knew a lot of them loved that moment when the victim realized, the eyes widening and shading with pure terror, mouth open with screams or words or just open in silent horror. Some dragged it out.

Ethel hated it, but this was a necessity for her. It was not fun. She did not enjoy this. It just was how it had to be. So when she dropped the guard, when she swooped toward his neck for that first delicious taste, she avoided his eyes. She did not want to see that moment of realization. She never did. This was survival.

And later that night, as she filled up the jar with her unique blend of lipstick, she sighed with relief. She had time before the next hunt. She could relax next weekend at the flea market. Maybe she could even take Ben up on that offer for coffee.

The End

Lady by Marge Simon

On this solstice night
I choose my best white frock
weave camellias in my hair,
open the cages of yesterday
to release my charges --
Robert and Maurice,
Claudia and little Jules.

With my silvery flute
I played you sweet songs,
and thus became your Lady.
As sister, mother, lover
I dressed & caressed
your dear warm bodies
satisfied your every need.

I took blood in payment
from each one of you,
slowly, and with due respect.
Now you follow like a pack
of hungry puppies, trusting
me still, and blind to the fact
that I own your souls.

Night Gallery

Breaking Ties

Review by the late Tom Johnson

- ➢ Title: Breaking Ties
- ➢ Author: Jo Grafford
- ➢ Genre: Historical Romance/Adventure & Survival
- ➢ ISBN: 978-1500379612
- ➢ Cost: $11.51 Paperback; $3.99 Kindle; 410 Pages
- ➢ Available at: Amazon, Barnes & Noble, and Google Books
- ➢ Rating: Five Stars

"A Wonderful Account of the Lost Colony."

When Rose Payne boards a ship heading for the New World, she's fleeing from a failed romance and seeking to put it far behind her. But she wasn't prepared for the danger and intrigue that awaited her as a clerk on board a ship bound for danger, leaving the colonists in a mysterious land where their survival is threatened by starvation and savage natives.

The first half of the book covers her journey on the sea with new friends she's met, as well as a handsome savage, bronzed and muscular, who sends her heart fluttering once more. Here we are introduced to the players in the story and the intrigue that holds their lives in the balance.

Sailing for Raleigh, on Chesapeake Bay, they are dropped instead on Roanoke Island. The second half of the book deals with the hardships on land as they try to survive amidst warring savages and the fast depletion of rations. Two men pursue her heart, one a British gentleman and the other a bronzed savage, but she can only choose one, and will they even survive to fulfill that love?

Written in first-person, it shows us the world through Rose's eyes. Some of it is violent, but it was an untamed period, and the violence in today's real world is much worse. Knowing the rough language of sailors, I was pleased that there was no profanity or sex, showing that a good book can be written without such to sell them. Based on a real event 500 years ago, the author gives us a well-written romanticized version of what *could* have happened. Her thorough research of the incident gives us a word-picture of the period and people, and we want to believe that some of it could really be true. Highly recommended for action readers as well as romance fans. The writing is smooth; the romance is light, and the action breathtaking.

Tom Johnson, Editor of *Echoes Magazine*

Omari and the People

Review by the late Tom Johnson

- ➢ Title: Omari And the People
- ➢ Author: Stephen Whitfield
- ➢ Genre: Epic Adventure
- ➢ Publisher: Sherlie Castle Press
- ➢ ISBN: 978-0964429031

- Cost: 12.10 Paperback; 366 pages
- Available at: Amazon, Barnes & Noble, and Google Books
- Rating: Four Stars

"In the Style of the Old Classic Adventure Literature."

In *The City*, located on the Sea of Providence, somewhere in the Empty Quarter of the Sahara Desert during the 13th Century, a rogue known as the Phantom Thief takes pleasure in robbing the wealthy ruling class. He lives high on his takings, as well, but has a good heart. An old woman in the square begs for food, which he buys for her when he visits the poor section. Returning to his home one night, he discovers that his wife has betrayed him and has revealed his identity to the authorities. As he burns his mansion, the fire also destroys *The City*. When he notices the old woman is still inside the flames, he rushes back to rescue her. Now he's tasked with leading the survivors of *The City* to a fabled Paradise somewhere in the desert.

Omari was that mysterious thief, a young rogue, good with a sword and tricks, who enjoyed stealing the government's tax money, even though he did not need it. But what, or who has chosen him to lead the exodus to the *Promised Land*? The handsome young rogue attracts the eye of a number of young women on the caravan, but he has fallen in love with Saba Khan, a warrior woman possessing some magic of her own, though the real magic belongs to the old woman he had saved from the fire.

This was a very interesting story, and kept my interest throughout. The characters were fascinating, the magic was brilliant, and the story telling was smooth. Truthfully, however, I felt that Omari the Phantom Thief was more interesting than Omari the caravan leader. And at times, the story does slow on the journey through the desert. This novel could have been serialized in *Argosy* or *Adventure* in the 1930s. There is no language, and sex is kept off screen. For anyone wishing to read a family adventure classic, I can highly recommend this book to you.

Tom Johnson, Editor of *Echoes Magazine*

Trail of Crosses

Review by the late Tom Johnson

- Title: Trail of Crosses
- Author: Jo Grafford
- Genre: Historical Romance/Action & Adventure)
- Book Two of The Lost Colony
- ASIN: B00NFGAEIQ; ISBN: 978-1944794057
- Price: $3.99 Kindle; $15.99 Paperback; 378 pages
- Available at: Amazon, Google Books, and Book Depository
- Rating: Five Stars

"Impossible to Put Down."

We first meet Jane Mannering in Book One, *Breaking Ties*, learning that she is a 23 or 24-year-old spinster, not catching men's eyes, nor wishing to. Tall and thin for a woman, she was raised as a hunter and trapper; she is equally skilled with a gun, bow, and knife, and can usually best any man. In fact, she carries three knives on her person at all times. I liked her immediately, as she reminded me Davy Crockett and many of our early tamers of the land. In this novel, she takes front stage. Captured by slavers in a savage attack, she and several companions are taken to a slave market to be sold. Chief Manteo, who was leading the colonists at the time, sends his cousin Chief Wanchese to rescue her.

Chief Wanchese has been smitten with the tall woman ever since the colonists' arrival, so he eagerly trails the slavers. Rescuing her and several others, he leads them back to his village instead of reuniting them with their fellow colonists. Given her independent nature, she refuses to adjust to the role of a woman, wishing to be recognized as a hunter, trapper, and fighter, but Chief Wanchese is determined to tame this proud woman and make her his mate. All this while, slavers and enemy tribes persist in causing problems; a fierce cyclone and smallpox plague the village, as well as unrest within the camp itself. Believe me, this is not just a romance novel; we have plenty of action, and the characterization is wonderful. I did get a chuckle when Jane kills a hooded cobra (native of Asia, not America) in the New World.

Most often, reality is harsher than fiction, but it's in our nature to hope terrible situations end with a positive outcome. Many rumors still contend that the Lost Colony was slaughtered by the indigenous peoples in the New World. However, some facts do remain to lead us in the opposite direction that some may have survived. During the early 17th Century to mid-18th Century, natives were found with light skin, blond hair, and blue eyes, a strong indication that the survivors of the Lost Colony intermingled with the local native tribes; many claimed their forbearers originally arrived from the sea in great boats. Whatever the truth of the 115 colonists that disappeared, we want to believe the best in their disappearance. Although Jo Grafford's novel is fiction, we can still hope that her romantic tale about the Lost Colony is at least partially true. This was a wonderful read, and I highly recommend it to readers of historical romance, and high adventure. There is never a dull minute in this great action/adventure novel of another period. There is one problem with the book, however - I didn't want to put it down!

Tom Johnson, Editor of *Echoes Magazine*

Inhuman Interest

Review by the late Tom Johnson

- ➤ Title: Inhuman Interest
- ➤ Genre: Horror
- ➤ Author: Eric Turowski
- ➤ Publisher: Booktrope Editions
- ➤ ISBN: 978-1620157992
- ➤ Price not listed; 204 Pages
- ➤ Available at: Amazon, Google Books, and other retailers
- ➤ Rating: Five Stars

"Intelligent and Well Written."

Tess Cooper is a full-time reporter, and part-time on the cop beat. When she's sent on an assignment to interview the "men on the street" for a human-interest feel-good story, she discovers possible city corruption instead. Or somebody is pretending to work for the city as they attempt to run businesses out of a mall. After bringing the story in, she's put on suspension for not doing the feel-good story for the paper. Looking for a temporary job, she runs across an ad in the newspaper, asking for an assistant immediately. Upon applying for the job, her life is suddenly turned upside down. Her new boss is Davin Egypt, and he is an occultist. Basically, he protects the city from occult things that pop up, and right now things are happening that even ties into the mall story and grave-yard robberies.

Tess is thrown into the middle of this gigantic case that is aimed at destroying her boss and the city on the anniversary of a devastating flood a hundred years in the past. It also involves giant bugs – centipedes under the control of occult powers.

This was a horror story with a touch of humor, as Tess stumbles into one situation after an-other, and very reminiscent of the old Kolchek TV series, but with a female lead in the part. Intelligent, and well written, the pace never lets up. Highly recommended.

Tom Johnson, Author of *Cold War Heroes*

Strange Loyalties

Review by the late Tom Johnson

- ➢ Title: Strange Loyalties
- ➢ Author: William McIlvanney
- ➢ Genre: Murder Mystery/Scottish Noir
- ➢ Publisher: Europa Editions www.europaeditions.com
- ➢ ISBN; 978-1609452537
- ➢ Price: $13.35 Paperback; 256 Pages
- ➢ Available at: Amazon, Google Books, and Book Depository
- ➢ Rating: Five Stars

Jack Laidlaw is trying to come to terms with his brother's death. Apparently, while drunk, Scott Laidlaw walked in front of a car, some saying suicide, others that it was just an accident; but Jack wants to find out what led up to that night and his brother's rendezvous with sudden death

His investigation starts uncovering problems in Scott's life, including a failed marriage and a mysterious night in college when Scott's life seemed to change to a darkness that Jack never sus-pected. While he's on a personal search, his police team is searching for a killer that may connect in some way back to Scott.

This was another interesting look into the Glasgow underworld where drugs and murder are the normal way of life and where Jack seems to be pulled deeper into its bottomless pit of darkness and inhuman savagery while his own family drifts apart. Although most of the story surrounds Jack's family and friends, the book kept my interest and is another deep look into the dark under-world of Glasgow. Highly recommended.

Tom Johnson, Editor of *Detective Mystery Stories*

The Three-Nine Line

Review by the late Tom Johnson

- ➢ Title: The Three-Nine Line
- ➢ Author: David Freed
- ➢ Genre: Murder Mystery "A Cordell Logan Mystery"

- Publisher: The Permanent Press www.thepermanentpress.com
- ISBN: 978-1579623999
- Price $29.00 Hardcover; 280 pages
- Available at: Amazon, Google Books, Audio Bookstore & other retailers
- Rating: Five Stars

"Well Written with a Good Twist."

Vietnam. Where Americans died. Where pilots were shot down and captured, spending years in captivity in the North's Hanoi Hilton, being tortured. Now America is seeking a Trade Agreement with Vietnam, and three ex-POWs are returning to Hanoi as good will ambassadors to cement the agreement. At a meeting, they are reunited with a vicious guard they nicknamed "Mr. Wonderful," who provided some of the more horrific torture. The former POWs are to let him know they no longer carry any grudge against him or Vietnam. But the next day, Mr. Wonderful is found murdered, and two ex-POWs are arrested for his murder.

The President wants an investigator sent to Hanoi to unravel the mystery and hopefully save the Trade Agreement. Cordell Logan, private pilot instructor, and ex-Alpha team assassin is called back into service. His old friend is now heading another unit, and he wants Logan to go to Hanoi, disguised as a psychiatrist named Bob Barker to act as the prisoners' doctor while in confinement.

This was a well-written mystery with a good twist. The setting was a good touch, and using ex-POWs as characters, though fictional, was a good plot tool. In 1973, I was part of security for Operation Welcome Home in California where families awaited aircraft bringing their heroes home. It's a time I'll never forget as those men stepped off the planes, and their families rushing through the security ropes to get to them. We wouldn't have stopped them if we wanted, and we didn't want to. We also guarded them at news conferences and in the hospital. Forty-two years ago, and you never hear about those heroes today. Even the war in Vietnam is almost forgotten. But this is a mystery story, and I highly recommend it to mystery lovers.

Tom Johnson, Author of *Detective Mystery Stories*

Double Trouble

Review by the late Tom Johnson

- Title: Double Trouble
- Author: Jerry Gill
- Genre: Action/Adventure
- Publisher: Ann Darrow Publishing
- ISBN: 978-150258829
- Price $12.54; 416 pages
- Available at: Amazon, Barnes & Noble, and Google Books
- Rating: Four Stars

"Old Style Fun & Adventure."

This actually contains the first two novels in the Vic Challenger series, "Time Doesn't Matter" and "Mongol." The first story has Victoria Custer and her brother, Barney, visiting Lord & Lady Greystoke's ranch in Africa, where Tarzan allows Vic to hunt water buffalo and other game. The natives and white men are all in awe of Vic, and Tarzan tells them that the girl is a capable hunter.

One day while Vic is out hunting, slavers capture her. Barney, Tarzan, and his Waziri take to the trail to rescue her and kill the Arab slavers. Amidst this early tale, Vic dreams about Nu and Nat-ul, a couple in love 100,000 years ago during the Stone Age. We learn their story, and how they influence Victoria Custer in 1919. In truth, Vic and Nat-ul seem to be attached, and Vic may be Nat-ul reincarnated. With this knowledge Vic feels she must find her lost lover, Nu, son of Nu, chief of the Nu people, dwellers in caves.

The story is episodic, with Vic falling into traps, escaping, fighting against great odds, and always showing the strength and fearlessness of the stone-age tribe of Nu. The author's writing style captures that of Edgar Rice Burroughs. And, indeed, we have the cameo of Tarzan at his African ranch, and chapter titles like "Back to the Stone Age," etc. In this story, Vic meets Ann Darrow who tells her about her adventure on Skull Island. She also meets an "Indiana" Jones. Victoria obtains a job with a big newspaper to supply stories and photographs of her adventures, using the byline of Vic Challenger, her homage to Professor Challenger from *The Lost World*.

In "Mongol," the second and weakest novel in the book, it reads a bit like a travelogue, with some episodic adventures. Lin Li, her pharmacist friend, joins Vic and they meet Evelyn Chan, the niece of Charlie Chan in San Francisco. She is a private detective involved in a murder mystery. The mystery follows them on board *The Red Dragon,* a ship heading for Hawaii before the mystery is solved. As they enter China, heading for Mongolia, they pick up a guide and learn about food and travel through the desert. They run across a band of Red Beards and have a shootout; then giant worms come out of the ground and attacks everyone. Then they discover an underground city with space aliens, and rooms filled with gold, jewels, and silver. Escaping seconds before being killed, they return to their guide's home to find Mongol warriors killing all the people. Alone, Vic, Lin, and their guide take on the Mongol horde in a fierce fight, defeating them just as the cavalry shows up.

Overall, this is a fun series so far, but the author needs to have better structure to the novel. Instead of short episodic adventures, the story needed a real plot the reader could follow. And with the travelogue in the second novel, the action slowed down a bit too much. For me, the story of Nu and Nat-ul, which took up a good portion of the first novel, was the best portion of the two books. The writing definitely captured Edgar Rice Burroughs in that segment. I like the character of Victoria Custer and Lin Li, although a lot of the dialogue was wooden in the second book. However, it is written in the old pulp style, and I think readers of adventure heroes like Doc Savage and Indiana Jones will enjoy it. Highly recommended.

Tom Johnson, Editor of *Echoes Magazine*

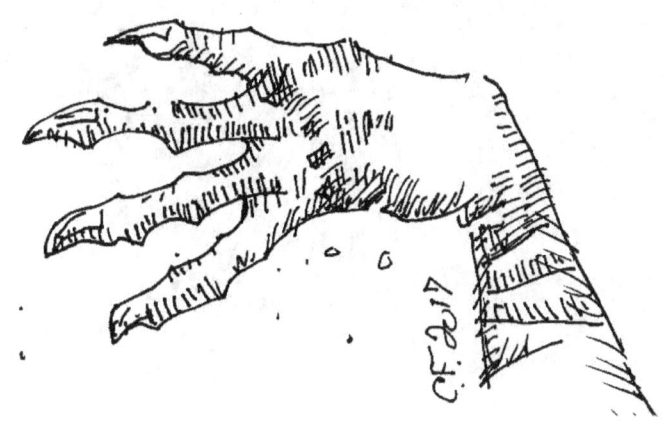

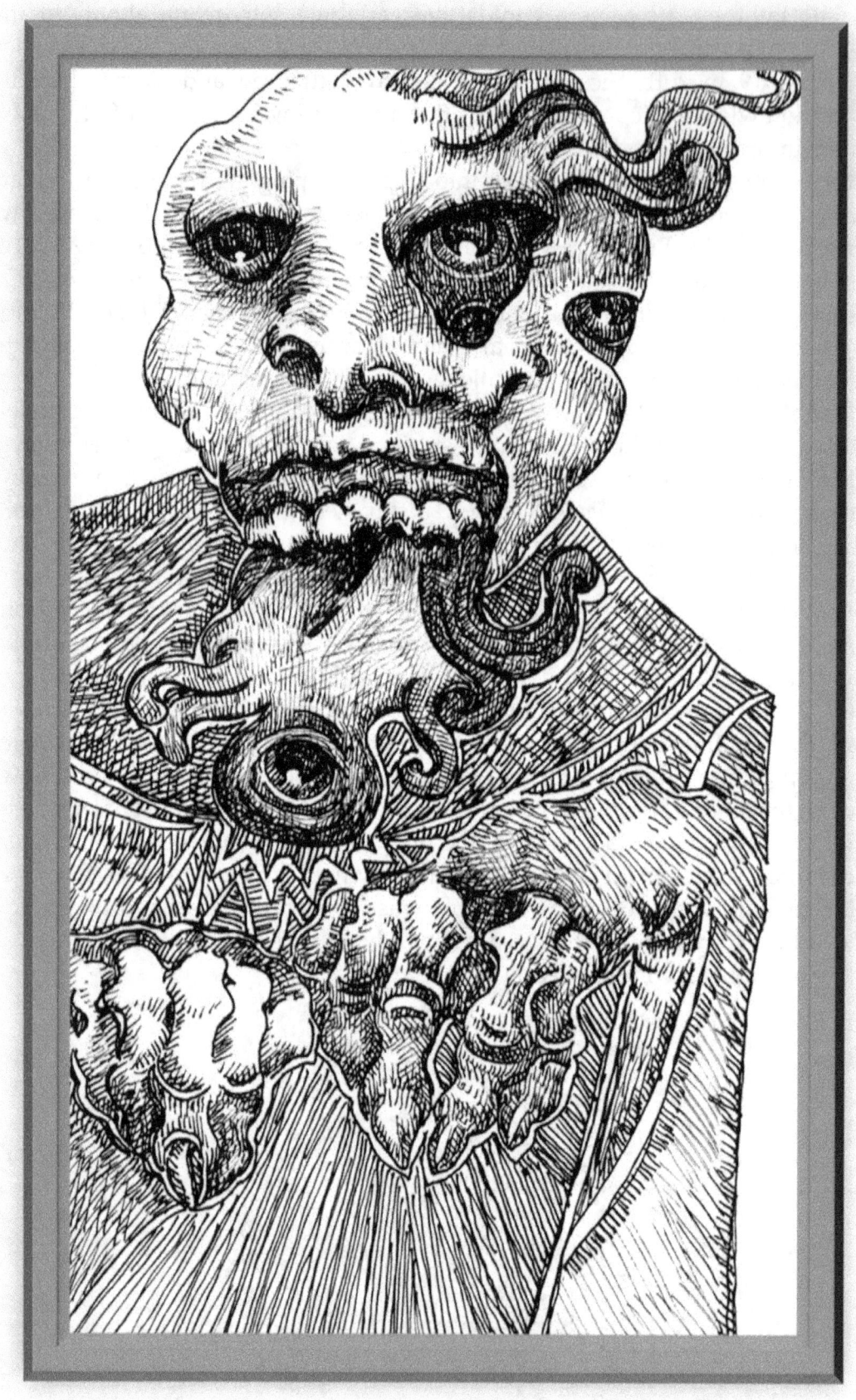

The Siren Lure
by
Barry Yedvobnick

Brody stopped hiking and stared at the brown and white mound, visible just ahead through the vegetation of the lowland Amazonian forest.

"Jas, you see that?" he asked.

"Yeah, I do. But I can't make out what it is from here," she replied.

Brody and Jas went far off-trail again, hoping to find something worth bringing back to the team at the research station. As they looked more carefully, their initial reaction was fear, not excitement.

"Human skeleton?" Brody said as they approached it nervously. They stopped about five feet from the tangle of dead brown vegetation that was now obviously intermixed with skeletal remains. There were some tattered clothes still attached to bones, along with a knife, machete, and some other equipment.

"This has been here a while," said Jas. As she crouched for a closer look, she noticed that several of the skeleton's ribs were broken, which she pointed out to Brody.

"Maybe fell and punctured a lung," he said.

Feeling nervous, he looked around cautiously and spotted something odd. Thicker brown tendrils of vegetation led from the skeleton, deeper into the adjacent undergrowth.

"That is weird. What do you make of it?" He used his machete to get a better look at the material.

"I have no idea, let's follow these," she said, pointing to the brown extensions.

They could now see that the tendrils extended further, and appeared to transition in color from brown to green about 20 feet from the skeleton.

"It looks like these lead to something alive," said Jas, shaking her head and giving Brody a confused glance.

As they followed the tendrils, Brody noticed a strange yet pleasant odor. He paused for a moment, looking around to find the source, and as he continued forward, the fragrance grew more intense.

"What's wrong?" asked Jas, noticing his pause.

"Kind of a strange odor out here, don't you think?" said Brody.

"Not really. Guess you've got a more sensitive nose than I do. I'm just picking up the usual," she said.

As Brody walked ahead, his anxiety about the skeleton disappeared, and he felt an unmistakable euphoria. Then he experienced a vivid déjà vu episode. He was back in high school with his girlfriend Olivia as they were having sex for the first time.

"Where did that come from?" Brody wondered to himself.

Though trying hard to concentrate, Brody realized that he was losing his focus. He found himself repeatedly thinking back to those exciting sexual sensations he had experienced with Olivia. Feeling disoriented, he poured some water into his hand and splashed his face briskly.

"You're looking a little unsteady Brody, are you feeling okay?" asked Jas, trailing several feet behind him.

Brody was about to answer, but as he parted more vegetation and looked ahead where several tendrils converged, he saw it.

"What the…,." he said as he stopped, refusing to believe what appeared before him.

"This is crazy, I'm hallucinating."

Twenty feet ahead of Brody appeared a naked woman, sitting in a small alcove of vegetation. She had long brunette hair, a perfectly symmetrical smiling face, and several other physical qualities that Brody found alluring. The odor, now even more intense, was emanating from her, but Brody no longer noticed it. His mind was now a mosaic of past sexual experiences, which coursed through his consciousness like a slideshow. As Brody stared at her, his heart rate accelerated and his desire soared. As Jas caught up to Brody, she noticed the woman.

"What in the name of God?" Jas asked. "Who the hell is that?"

"Are you okay?" Brody asked the woman, not listening to Jas and straining to clear his head. There was no response, so he moved closer to her.

"Hold on a minute Brody," said Jas, as she grabbed his arm. "Let's think about this. Something is not right here."

"Do you need some help?" he asked, as he pulled away from Jas and kept walking.

As he brushed aside some thin branches that stood between them, she rotated slowly towards him, with no change in her expression. Brody found her irresistible and gently touched her hair and shoulder. She felt abnormally cold and damp, but that did not affect him as he caressed her face. As he felt himself losing self-control, he moved closer and pressed his body against her.

"What the hell are you doing, Brody, you can't do that!" yelled Jas. She rushed towards Brody, grabbing his arm again, attempting to pull him away. But Brody refused to move, and violently pushed her back. She fell over, striking the ground hard.

"Who are you?" he asked the woman as he placed his face against her neck and closed his eyes.

Her arms rose and wrapped around him, her fingers pressing along his back. Probing fingers moved to the midline of his back, settling into the grooves of his backbone. As Brody held on to her tightly, thorn-like tips on her fingers penetrated deeply through his skin and broke through the membranous layer enclosing his spinal cord. Brody screamed and arched backward, instinctively attempting to move away, but her arms held him tightly, crushing several ribs. Neurotoxins pumped from the thorns, immobilizing Brody's lower body.

"Oh my God, Brody!" shouted Jas as she jumped up off the ground and ran to him. She grabbed his shirt and belt buckle and pulled back as hard as she could, but the woman held on too tightly for her to free him.

As Brody moaned and struggled to push the woman away, her fingers moved up his back to the cervical vertebrae of his neck, where more neurotoxins were injected. Brody then stopped struggling and lost consciousness, as numerous thin green tendrils descended upon him and Jas. The thorny tendrils rapidly wrapped themselves around Brody's body and injected a cocktail of digestive enzymes.

"Brody," screamed Jas as she unsheathed her knife and plunged it deep into the woman's head several times. The blade pierced through but had no effect. Jas's arms and upper body were now covered by the tendrils, and she felt the sensation of a thousand bee stings. As the thorns injected enzymes throughout her body, she fell to the ground, unconscious.

Over the next 18 hours, Jas and Brody's tissues were reduced to a nutrient soup and transported to new growth regions of the plant. Three days later, the original plant was dead, intertwined with their skeletons. It had produced two identical offspring, some distance away in the thick foliage.

****

The student turned from the video and looked at her committee of examiners.

"Where did you get the idea for this mimic as a sexual lure for the human male?" asked examiner one. "The combination of pheromones and the visual attraction was ingenious."

"I got that idea from a plant found on Earth in Australia," said the student.

"It is called a Hammer Orchid, and it uses mimicry to attract male wasps to assure pollination. The Orchid develops a structure that resembles a female wasp, and the male actually attempts to mate with it, thereby picking up or depositing pollen. The Orchid also releases insect pheromones to attract the male wasps, so I incorporated both attractants into my project."

"Your technical work here is commendable," said examiner two, "but it is time to move on to the problem with this project. Tell us what went wrong and why."

"Something unexpected happened with the mimic plant on Earth;" she replied.

"Several flowered and formed seeds before we could clear them from test sites. Many seeds were disseminated in the rainforest, and those that germinated in vibrant environments developed fully into mimics using only soil nutrients, rather than through the carnivorous route."

"And the consequences?" asked examiner two.

"Instead of just a few mimics, several thousand developed," she said.

"Unfortunately, there was a significant loss of human life. It has been contained there now, but I suspect some seeds have been more widely spread by birds and other wildlife. I expect the problem for Earth is not over."

****

As the student was finishing the presentation, Aaron was opening his water bottle and resting in the shade on the Palmetto Trail in South Carolina. He loved hiking and cycling, and this trail afforded both over its 425 miles.

While Aaron rested, he used his senses to take in the moment. The scent of a forest was among his favorites. A warm wind touched his face and evaporated the perspiration, and he could discern the usual odors. But there was something different in the air here.

"What is that!" he wondered. After several minutes, a slight breeze drifted in from the west, and the fragrance intensified.

"That way," he said, "let's check this out."

The End

Aitvaras by Lee Clark Zumpe

he skulks behind the hearth,
a tangle of shadows
sheathed in a sable satin coat
punctuated by two copper eyes,
purring seductively while
evaluating potential acquisitions –
charming children, enticing the elderly,
haggling for a handful of souls

Author's Note: The Aitvaras is "a Lithuanian household spirit which appears as a black cat," and which "persuades the householder to sell his soul for a rich reward."
Source: Lurker, Mandred. Dictionary of Gods and Goddesses, Devils and Demons. New York: Routledge, 1996.

Homecoming in Ostrava, 1995
by
Lee Clark Zumpe

Adrian Iliescu examined a fading crimson strip etched into the chimney smoke along the western horizon. Standing amidst the gray trunks of dead trees on a mountainside near Ostrava, Adrian winced at the stench of sulfur smothering the once lush forest.

In the distance, smelting works painted the dusk with a grubby orange glow.

"I don't like coming home." Bogdon, disaffiliating himself from the leaden shadows, startled Adrian.

"I find I cannot leave."

"I saw the town – the rows of dingy houses and filthy tenements. They live like animals in blackened holes."

"They know nothing else."

"Adrian," Bogdon gripped the older man's arm and shook him gently, "Come with me – come to America. I'll show you the Appalachian Mountains."

"I cannot..."

"Anya's been gone for two hundred years ... you have to let her go."

"No." Adrian turned away from his only child. "I know nothing else."

The End

Werewolf Watch
by
Margaret L. Carter

"Your newest patient is a werewolf?" Roger Darvell arched his eyebrows at Dr. Britt Loren, his partner in both psychiatry and life.

Eating lunch, a fruit-and-yogurt parfait, on her office couch, she paused between spoonfuls. "Why does that come as a shock? I've had one before."

He leaned against the desk, sipping from the mug of triple-strength coffee that he relied on to stay alert at a time of day when his natural circadian rhythm would have dictated sleep. "Yes, but that was years ago, and I didn't expect you to make a habit of it. What's next, zombies?"

"Zombies don't have brains, so we wouldn't be able to analyze them anyway."

He sighed at her attempt at humor. "Since they don't exist—I hope—it's a moot point." Despite being a vampire himself, or, technically, half-vampire, he remained skeptical of the existence of other legendary beings. After all, his kind weren't supernatural. Like werewolves, they were merely a different humanoid species or subspecies. "How did you happen to acquire another werewolf?"

"My former patient recommended me to him. Technically, he's a human-werewolf hybrid, like her. He gave me permission to consult you about his case."

"What's his problem?" Roger sat on the couch, far enough from Britt that he could resist touching her. Physical contact might tempt him to behavior that would be unprofessional in the middle of a work day.

"He's afraid he's been attacking people. He's seen news articles that have him worried, even though he doesn't remember doing anything of the kind."

"So he thinks he might transform and go on rampages while suffering blackouts?"

"That's essentially it." She scraped the inside of the cup and licked yogurt from the spoon.

Roger forcibly dragged his gaze away from her lips and tongue. Not that focusing on the appetizing glow of her aura or the gleam of filtered sunlight on her golden-red hair was much better. He took a sip of the hot coffee, a far from adequate substitute for what he craved. *Keep your mind on the work!* "What did you have in mind, then?"

"I'm hoping that if his fear has any basis in reality, you could dig out the truth by hypnosis." She took a last bite of fruit and set the container aside. "If that wouldn't stress you too much."

"Not with a male subject." Even though he was bonded with and permanently fixated on Britt, mesmerizing women still tended to rouse his appetite. "The scenario he's concerned about isn't impossible. Your other werewolf suffered a similar problem, didn't she?"

Britt nodded. "At least this guy has known his true nature all along, unlike her. He has a human father and a werewolf mother. They're divorced, and I get the impression that the man's inability to deal with the lycanthropic lifestyle was the main cause of the breakup. They had twin boys, barely a year old at the time, and the father got custody of my patient's brother."

Roger took another meditative drink of his coffee. "Does he have regular contact with them?"

"Regular but rare, basically a short visit every Christmas. It sounds like a strained situation."

"No wonder." He knew all too well the difficulties of balancing the two halves of a mixed-species heritage. Glancing at his watch, he stood up. Their one o'clock patients would be arriving soon. "Well, let me know when you want that joint session, and I'll shuffle my schedule." The two of them had no more information about wolf-shifters than Britt had been able to glean from observing her previous patient, so he looked forward to the intellectual challenge offered by this new one.

****

Two days later, they met to "tag-team the werewolf," as Britt put it. The patient, Carlos Reye, offered his hand as Roger strode into his partner's office. The young man, apparently in his early twenties, had olive skin, curly, black hair, and the characteristic lycanthropic trait of bushy eyebrows that met over the nose. Unlike Roger, who as a vampire had the same feature, Carlos didn't minimize that anomaly by shaving between his brows. Darker crimson streaks in the rose-pink of his aura hinted at his nonhuman heritage, as did a wild tinge in his scent. His nostrils flared, as if he'd noticed the metallic aroma that signaled Roger's hybrid nature. Since he had no idea vampires existed, of course, that oddity would puzzle him. When they shook hands, Roger noticed the other inescapable sign of lycanthropy, index and middle fingers of the same length.

"Thanks in advance for your help," Carlos said as Britt waved him to a seat on the couch. His pulse, audible to Roger's superhuman hearing, raced with tension. "You don't have any trouble believing I'm a werewolf?"

"I trust Dr. Loren's judgment." He rolled the desk chair over to sit facing the patient, while Britt positioned herself on the other end of the couch. "She's given me a summary of your problem, but please tell me about it in your own words."

The young man knotted his fingers together. "I'm afraid I might be changing at night without knowing it and hurting people."

With a light touch on Carlos' wrist, Roger applied a subtle psychic nudge to calm him. "What makes you think that?"

"Reports of animal attacks the day after I've had nightmares about turning into a wolf against my will. I haven't seen any evidence that I've left the house, but that doesn't necessarily mean anything, does it?"

"Up until now, have you had control over your transformations?" Contrary to popular culture clichés, werewolf shifting had no connection to the phases of the moon. If a subject believed that superstition, though, the belief might have psychosomatic consequences.

Carlos shrugged. "As far as I know. When I'm awake, I can still turn from human to wolf and back at will. I go hunting in the woods—just animals like rabbits, deer, raccoons—two or three nights a week to get the urge out of my system."

"Alone?" Britt asked.

"Yeah, except when I first started and Mom was training me. She doesn't belong to a pack, so I've never wanted to get into that scene." From what little Roger and Britt knew about werewolf packs, they might object to associating with human-werewolf hybrids.

"How can I be sure I'm not transforming in sleep?" A dimming of Carlos' aura mirrored the strain in his voice.

"How many times has this happened?" Roger asked.

"Four over the past few weeks."

"Have you asked your mother for advice?"

The patient shook his head with a sheepish expression. "I don't want to worry her. Plus, I'm kind of ashamed to admit I might be losing control after she tried so hard to teach me how to handle my condition. That's why I decided to go to a psychiatrist instead. I dropped some hints about my trouble to Jenny." That was Britt's former werewolf patient. "She recommended Dr. Loren, so here I am." He nodded at Britt. "She said maybe you could find out what's going on by hypnotizing me."

"Is that what you want?"

"Yes, if it'll get to the bottom of this." His heartbeat accelerated again despite the assumed confidence in his tone.

"It may," Roger said. "Regardless, your nervousness is natural, but there's no need for it. Contrary to popular belief, hypnosis doesn't turn you into a helpless puppet." Vampiric mesmerism, actually, could have that effect, but of course, he wouldn't think of exerting that kind of control in this situation.

"Will I remember what I say and do while I'm in a trance?"

"*Trance* is an imprecise word. Think of it as a state of induced relaxation. Do you want to remember?"

An emphatic nod.

"Then you can." With another fleeting touch, Roger willed the young man's frantic pulse to slow down. "Shall we go ahead with it now?"

Carlos let out a long breath. "Might as well get it over with. I can't stand not knowing."

"Very well. Dr. Loren, could we have the blinds closed?" She got up to do so, then returned to her seat. Roger suppressed a sigh of relief at having the glare of the sun blocked. "Now, look directly at me. Focus on my eyes," he said to Carlos.

"Aren't you going to dangle a shiny object in front of me or something?"

Roger replied with a wry smile, "That's not necessary. This isn't a stage performance, and I'm not going to make you bark like a dog—or howl like a wolf."

Carlos managed a weak grin in return.

"Look into my eyes and take long, deep breaths. In and out, yes, like that." He rested a hand on the young man's wrist, transmitting his will through the light contact. "In through the nose, out through the mouth. You are becoming deeply relaxed. Nothing can harm you. You will remember everything I tell you to remember but without emotion. No agitation, no fear. Understand?"

"Yes," Carlos whispered.

Roger continued the soothing touch and murmured commands until he sensed the subject drifting into the tranquil, passive state of complete openness to suggestion. "Cast your mind back to the last time you suffered one of those nightmares. Remember, that cannot hurt you. It is already in the past. When did it happen?"

"Earlier this week, Monday night." The young man spoke in a low monotone.

"Tell me about the nightmare. How did it begin?"

"I found myself in a grove of trees, as a wolf. It came as a shock because the last thing I remembered was going to bed. Don't know how I got there. I felt dizzy."

"You were disoriented."

"Yeah."

"But you got your bearings?" Roger spoke with confidence that he hoped would transmit itself to the patient.

A sluggish nod. "I could see the moon through the trees, half full. Smelled pine trees and animal scents."

"Did you know where you were?"

Carlos shook his head. "I started running. After a while, I figured out I must be in some kind of park. There wasn't a lot of underbrush around the trees, and there were paths."

"And then?"

"A deer ran across the path, so I chased it. It sprinted into the trees and I lost it."

"How did you feel then?"

The patient's pulse accelerated again, and he bared his teeth. "Frustrated. Hungry. Then I caught a human scent. Started tracking it." His breath quickened.

"Calm," Roger murmured. "This is only a memory."

Carlos released a long, shuddering breath. "I smelled a man. Young man on the path ahead. I broke into a run. He started running, too." His fists clenched in his lap, and his throat convulsed as he visibly swallowed. "I caught up with him. Leaped on his back and knocked him down." A growl rumbled in his chest. A thread of saliva dribbled from one corner of his mouth. Dark fuzz began to spread over his forehead and cheeks like a layer of moss. Even his scent subtly changed.

Touching his shoulder, Roger said in a sterner tone, "Control yourself. This isn't happening now. It's in the past. You can restrain your inner wolf."

The young man's lips curled back from teeth that had sharpened. Roger heard Britt's pulse race in alarm, along with Carlos' pounding heart. "You don't have to become the beast. You can still think and speak. What did you do to your victim?"

Panting, Carlos answered in a hoarse voice, "Bit his shoulder through his shirt. I smelled fear, tasted sweat and blood. He screamed. I heard footsteps running toward me."

"What did you do?"

"Don't know. Everything went black."

"That's enough. The beast will go to sleep now. You are yourself again."

In response to Roger's commands and firm touch, the hair disappeared, the teeth reverted to normal, and the patient's pulse and breathing slowed. "You will come to full consciousness now and remember everything you've told me." He slowly counted backward from ten to one.

Carlos closed his eyes, unclenched his fist, and sighed. When he opened his eyes, Roger asked, "What was the next thing you recalled after that scene?"

"Waking up at five a.m." He scrubbed a hand across his face. "That day, I searched the Internet and found a news item about a man who got attacked by a feral dog—so he said—in a park in Baltimore."

Britt fetched him a paper cup of water from the cooler in a corner of the room. "And you live in Glen Burnie, don't you?" That area was in the northern part of Anne Arundel County, adjacent to Baltimore.

"Yeah. Not too far for a wolf to roam in an hour or two." He gulped the water and crushed the cup in his fist.

Roger leaned back in his chair. "Did you find any concrete evidence that you'd done so?"

Carlos shook his head. "No grass, dirt, or leaves in the bedroom. The window and door were shut. But that doesn't prove anything."

"Granted," Britt said. "Absence of evidence doesn't equal evidence of absence, or in this case, non-occurrence."

"No victims have died, have they?" Roger asked. Although he already knew that from Britt, he wanted to emphasize the fact for the patient's sake.

"No, but who knows how long I'll be that lucky?"

Britt frowned thoughtfully. "Have you considered setting up a camera or other recording equipment?"

"It did cross my mind, but I haven't done anything about it. Anyway, if I could lock the doors and windows after prowling outside and not realize I'd done it, I could shut off a camera without remembering it, too."

"True, the unconscious mind can be devious," Britt said. "Then what you need is somebody to watch you overnight. Have you noticed a pattern to the timing of these episodes?"

"Actually, it's been completely predictable. Every seventh night."

"Then maybe it's related to the phases of the moon." Britt held up a hand to silence him when he started to interrupt. "Yes, I know lycanthropy doesn't depend on the full moon, contrary to the movies. But does your unconscious mind know that?"

Carlos shrugged. "The inside of my head is a mystery to me. That's your department."

"According to that schedule," Roger asked, "the next incident should occur this coming Monday."

The patient nodded.

Britt asked, "Will you agree to having us spend Monday night keeping watch over you?"

"You make house calls?"

She smiled. "In special circumstances like this, yes."

"Sure, you can come over. But wouldn't that be dangerous for you guys? I wouldn't want to risk hurting you."

Roger and Britt exchanged a look, coming to a silent agreement. "Don't concern yourself about that," he said. "There will be two of us, after all, and we'll be prepared."

As the young man got up to leave, he broadcast relief, probably at having put his problem in the hands of competent professionals.

After he'd gone, Britt asked with a wry smile, "If we do catch him transforming and attacking people, what next?"

"Granted, we can hardly report him to the police."

"Just saying 'bad werewolf, no biscuit' doesn't seem like an adequate solution." Mulling over the problem, she drummed her fingers on the edge of the desk. "Hmm—could you suppress the involuntary metamorphosis with a deeper hypnotic trance?"

"Maybe. How can we know, since I've never dealt with this syndrome before? It's worth a try."

"Yeah." She headed for the door to prepare for her next patient. "Let's hope it won't come to that."

****

They made arrangements to meet Carlos at his home the following Monday at ten p.m. They drove separate cars in case they needed both for a flexible response to the patient's behavior. Roger still felt energized from their Sunday night together, while Britt, more of a day person, had taken an early evening nap before setting out. Carlos lived in a one-story condo at the end of a four-unit row. A compact front yard held a small patch of closely mown grass and, under the picture window, three azalea bushes. A high, wooden fence surrounded the back of the lot.

With a nervous handshake for each of them, he let them in. His pulse raced in Roger's ears. When asked to show the doctors around, Carlos said, "Sure, there's not much to it." The living room, an eat-in kitchen, two bedrooms—one furnished as an office—a bathroom attached to the master bedroom, and another in the hall. The flat-screen TV and game systems connected to it, in contrast to the worn, saggy couch and armchair, betrayed the resident's preference for comfort and entertainment over elegance. The aromas of hamburgers and fries lingered in the air along with the background odors of human occupation.

They finished the tour in Carlos' bedroom. "If I'm sleepwalking and leaving the house," he said, "it's probably this way." He gestured at the window that looked onto the fenced patio. "When I prowl on purpose, I go out the kitchen door into the yard here, where nobody can see me strip down and change. I leave the gate ajar so I can get back in."

"How often do you roam at large as a wolf?" Britt asked.

"That I'm aware of? Weekend nights, usually all three, Friday through Sunday. I go to a wooded area nearby to hunt."

Gazing at the dark patio through the open window curtains, Roger said, "Then you shouldn't suffer from frustrated predatory urges that would drive you to transform involuntarily." He turned to face the young man. "Set your mind at ease. We'll get to the bottom of this."

Carlos' heartbeat became more sedate in response to the reassurance Roger projected, but his tone remained dubious. "What if I'm suppressing frustrated urges to kill people instead of animals?"

"No need to borrow trouble by making unfounded assumptions," Britt said. "For what it's worth, I haven't noticed anything in our sessions to indicate you're harboring such drives."

Having previously discussed how they would handle the night watch, Roger and Britt laid out their plan. He would stay in the bedroom with the patient, while she would rest in the living room until her help was needed, if at all. They didn't explain the details, since they couldn't tell Carlos that if he started to transform, Roger would trail him on foot while alerting Britt telepathically. If she fell asleep, Roger could wake her with a psychic touch. She would follow in her car, keeping in mental contact with him.

While she settled on the couch with a book, he carried a kitchen chair into the bedroom, furnished with only the bed, a dresser, and a laundry hamper. Carlos emerged from the bathroom in boxer shorts and a ragged T-shirt. "Sorry it's not more comfortable in here."

Roger waved away the apology. "Is this your usual bedtime?"

"Close enough. I wake up early on weekdays to commute into D.C. But I might be too nervous to fall asleep."

"I should be able to remedy that problem."

The young man turned down the covers and lay on his back, hands clasped behind his head. "Oh, yeah, the hypnotism thing. Come to think of it, couldn't you hypnotically order me not to change?"

"That might work short-term. However, I could hardly visit you every night to reinforce the command, so you need a permanent solution." Roger walked to the bedside. "Are you ready now?"

"Sure, go for it." The strain in Carlos' voice belied the casual statement. "Hey—if you do see me about to attack a person—"

"Needless to say, we won't allow you to hurt anybody." Fortunately, Carlos didn't ask how they planned to stop him. "That position creates too much tension in your arm muscles. Move your arms to your sides. Don't curl the fingers. Relax them. Now, breathe slowly from the diaphragm and let yourself go limp. Fingers and toes first, then arms and legs…"

When the young man had completely relaxed, Roger commanded him to sleep. Five minutes later, Roger sat in the straight-backed chair and made himself as comfortable as possible in the circumstances. Without knowing what time of night the incidents usually occurred, he prepared himself for what might be a long wait. The window let in a trace of light from a street lamp on the corner, enough illumination for Roger, with his nocturnally adapted vision, to read the paperback mystery he'd brought along.

Less than an hour later, a faint noise diverted his attention from the fictional detective's deductions. On the bed, Carlos' chest rumbled with a barely audible growl. His aura darkened to a turgid crimson. Apparently still asleep, he curled his lips to expose teeth sharpening to fangs.

Getting up to stand over the bed, Roger telepathically alerted Britt. *He's agitated, but so far, he hasn't changed any further than he did at our consultation.*

Well, be careful.

There's nothing to worry about yet. If he does transform, he's not likely to attack me, and I could handle him if he did.

Oh, yeah? Her mental "voice" felt half-anxious and half-amused. *We've never done any tests to calibrate the comparative strengths of werewolves and vampires.*

Meanwhile, dark fuzz sprouted on Carlos' face. It spread like a rising tide over his torso and arms, then receded until it shaded only his cheeks. His fingernails elongated into claws. As his snarls grew louder, his scent altered to the musk of a wild beast. His heartbeat raced. Yet he changed no further and didn't try to leave the bed. Instead, he grimaced and thrashed as if in pain.

This is so distressing to watch. I'm almost tempted to wake him.

Almost? Britt countered.

We can't draw a definite conclusion this quickly. We have to know for sure whether he's prowling outside.

Roger stared at the writhing man for fifteen minutes. The fangs and claws lengthened and shortened, while the layer of fur expanded and retreated over and over. *Enough. He hasn't made any move toward getting up.* He touched Carlos' forearm.

The young man arched his back and snapped like a feral dog. Roger got a firm grip on Carlos' arm and said, "You will wake up now. Lie still and rise slowly to consciousness. All is well."

The patient's breathing calmed under the pressure of Roger's will. Carlos' limbs went limp, his pulse slowed, and the fuzz disappeared along with the fangs and claws. A sheen of sweat coated his skin. "You are safe. All is well. Open your eyes."

Carlos obeyed. He blinked a few times, then stared up at Roger, who let go of his arm. "Huh? I'm here?"

Roger took a step back while the patient sat up. "Where did you think you were?"

"In that same park, trailing a human scent." He rubbed his chin as if expecting to feel animal hair. "It was so real. I was *there*. But I wasn't, was I?"

"No, you never left this bed. I suggest you compose yourself, and then we'll discuss it." When Carlos headed for the attached bathroom, Roger withdrew to the living room.

Britt stood up. "So he's not prowling the night or even fully changing, unless tonight was an anomaly. Then why has he been experiencing it as if he did?"

"Suppose he has a psychic link to the actual perpetrator of those incidents?"

"I think I know what you're getting at."

When Carlos trudged into the living room, Roger said, "We're considering an explanation for what you're going through. We'll stay a while longer until you've fallen asleep again and we can be fairly certain you won't leave the house, but it seems likely you have nothing to worry about on that score."

He slumped into the chair, while the two doctors sat on the couch opposite him. "Then what's going on?"

"We suspect you're telepathically picking up the sensations of the real attacker," Roger said.

With a puzzled frown, the young man straightened up. "You guys believe in that ESP stuff?"

Britt smiled. "Any stranger than believing in werewolves?"

"So you think there's another werewolf in the local area, and I'm mentally sharing his transformation? How?"

"Think about it," Roger said, "and you'll realize there's one likely explanation. Dr. Loren mentioned that you have a twin brother."

"Oh." Carlos' eyes widened as if he'd been hit between them. "So you think my brother Miguel might be a werewolf?"

"Don't you know?" she asked.

He shrugged. "We've never discussed it. We're friends on Facebook, but I can't casually drop a comment about moonlight and fur between cat videos. Other than that, about the only contact we have is holiday visits. The way Dad feels about the whole werewolf thing, it's not something I want to bring up when I see them. After all, that's why he left Mom in the first place."

Britt said, "I'd be surprised if your twin weren't like you in that respect. You're identical?"

The young man nodded.

"If we can draw conclusions from a very small sample, it seems probable that the gene for lycanthropy is dominant." As Roger knew, she'd been baffled by the fact that her female werewolf patient's father but not her paternal grandparents had displayed the condition—until the patient's discovery that her father had been adopted.

Roger leaned back against the desk, arms folded. "Would you feel comfortable approaching your brother on this subject now?"

"Not exactly comfortable. How am I supposed to ask him out of the blue if he's been attacking pedestrians in parks?" Carlos scrubbed a hand across his face. "But I guess I'll have to." He hesitated before continuing in a tentative voice, "If I can talk him into coming to your office, could you guys discuss it with both of us together?"

Roger nodded, and Britt said, "We'd be glad to. Just contact me as soon as you've arranged it with him."

The patient sighed and stretched. "If you really think I'm not sleepwalking—or sleep-hunting—I feel better already. Maybe I could actually get a decent night's rest for a change."

****

The following afternoon, Britt told Roger that Carlos had persuaded his brother to talk to them. Miguel Reye balked at coming to the psychiatrists' office, though. Britt's patient asked whether the two doctors would be willing to meet at his condo again. After confirming the details of date and time, Britt hung up the phone and faced Roger with a wry smile. "We may be setting a bad precedent with all these house calls."

"Our not-quite-human patients aren't likely to discuss their treatment with casual acquaintances," he said, "so I doubt we have to worry about the word getting around."

On Thursday around sunset, they drove together in Roger's car to Carlos' home. When he let them in, he said, "Miguel's out back. He said he felt trapped inside."

"Whatever makes both of you comfortable is fine," Britt said. She and Roger followed their host through the house into the tiny yard with its patio surrounded by a narrow rim of grass and the six-foot-tall, wooden privacy fence. A couple of lightning bugs flickered under an azalea bush, and the humid evening breeze carried the fragrance of newly mown lawns. In the middle of the patio stood another man with Carlos' olive skin, brown eyes, and black hair. His hair was longer than his twin's, though, almost to his collar, and shaggy with uneven bangs. He hadn't trimmed his bushy eyebrows at all, and he emitted a musky aroma that a human observer might not have noticed, but Roger couldn't miss.

He seems — wilder — than Carlos, Roger silently noted to Britt.

She projected silent agreement. *Maybe a reaction against trying too hard to suppress that side of his nature?*

I can identify with that. Roger had spent twenty years of his life struggling to do the same before he'd learned the truth about his vampire heritage. After Carlos made the introductions, Roger strode up to Miguel and offered his hand. The other man shook it as quickly as possible and backed off with a visible flinch. *Afraid of losing control even here?*

"You guys know about all that supernatural stuff? And you believe it?"

Roger nodded, taking a seat in one of several lawn chairs along with Britt and Carlos. "It's not technically supernatural, though. You and your mother and brother belong to a naturally evolved human subspecies."

Instead of settling down, Miguel paced back and forth across the patio. "How do you know?"

"Those details are confidential." Britt softened the remark with a soothing smile. "After all, you wouldn't want us to discuss your case with anyone else, would you?"

"Right." He raked his fingers through his hair. "Carlos said you think I'm randomly turning into a wolf and he's picking it up telepathically."

"Twins do sometimes have psychic bonds," Britt said. "That phenomenon has been reliably documented. Now that Carlos has told you about his nocturnal visions, I'd be surprised if you haven't checked online to confirm the incidents you mentally shared."

The young man's shoulders sagged. "Yeah. The times match up with the nightmares I've been having myself. At least, I thought they were just nightmares." He glowered at them. "But I shouldn't be changing."

Roger captured his gaze. "Indeed? Why not?"

"Because I don't let myself." The words came out almost as a growl. "I don't have to be a werewolf just because my mother was." He cast a sharp glance at his brother. "Or you. I didn't show any signs until all this started. I figured that meant I'd escaped."

"You're half-human," Britt said. "It's not surprising that the age of onset might be unpredictable."

"When I started feeling the urges, I fought them. I don't want to be a savage beast."

Carlos frowned. "Hey, I'm not savage, and neither is Mom."

Britt held up a hand to silence them. "Miguel, did your father suggest that to you?"

"Not in so many words. But he's never made a secret of his attitude. He wants me to be human. I tried not to let him down."

"You could hardly change your inborn nature," Roger said. Although Carlos kept his face blank, Roger sensed his distress. *No doubt, he couldn't be unaware of his father's disappointment that he grew up as a "beast" instead of human.*

Britt silently agreed. *Must make those Christmas dinners awkward.* Aloud, she said, "You are human, just a different variety of human. You have a dual heritage, both sides equally valid."

Leaning against the fence, Miguel sighed heavily. "Tell that to Dad."

Carlos stood up and patted his shoulder. "You don't have to tell him anything you don't want to, you know. Hell, I don't make a habit of mentioning things he doesn't need to hear."

With a thin smile, his twin said, "I've noticed."

Britt said, "Miguel, do you know why your lycanthropic tendencies break out this way while your brother's don't?"

He shrugged. "I'm sure you're going to tell me." When she remained silent, he said, "Because I don't practice the way Carlos does? Is that why I can't control it?"

"Partly, I'm sure, but there's a more basic reason."

"Like what?" With a hint of a snarl, he started pacing again. "Come on, you're the experts."

"Struggling to deny that part of yourself causes you to repress the need to change. Naturally, it's going to erupt when you least expect or want it. Nothing like that can be leashed indefinitely."

He winced at the "leash" reference. "So do you have a cure for me?"

"We wouldn't use the word *cure*, as if your essential nature were a disease," Roger said. "What you can learn to do is control your werewolf side, express it when you choose to instead of against your will."

70

"Like he does?" Miguel gestured at Carlos. "He told me it helped when you hypnotized him. Could you control my change that way?"

"It might help *you* control it, but that wouldn't take the place of your own efforts."

"The fact is, I'm scared." His aura darkened. "I've hurt people. It's just dumb luck that I haven't killed anybody."

Roger caught his gaze and projected calm. "In my experience, so-called 'luck' usually isn't. Your desire to avoid harming human victims may have restrained you, even when you assumed you were dreaming. Also, the psychic link with your twin may have reined in your predatory drive, even without conscious awareness of that link."

"One root of your problem," Britt said, "might be that you've tried to handle it on your own. Werewolves aren't meant to be solitary predators."

Unlike vampires, Roger thought. "From what little we've learned about your kind, that's true. A lone wolf is more likely to be dangerous to himself and others."

"What, you think I should join a pack?" Miguel bristled, his lips curling back to expose his teeth. "No, thanks!"

"I wouldn't go for that, either," Carlos said. "But I wouldn't mind having somebody to run with. Now that I know you're the same as me—well, we could keep an eye on each other."

"Yeah?" His brother's bristling eyebrows arched. "You think that would keep me out of trouble?"

"Keep both of us out of trouble. Maybe getting hypnotized by Dr. Darvell would put us in the right mindset."

Roger nodded. "That sounds like a productive approach. We can help you exploit the advantages of that link you share."

Carlos grinned. "What have we got to lose? I've always thought our folks were wrong to separate us, and now I know it."

"True that." Miguel flashed a smile in return. "Our own private mini-pack? Okay, I'm ready to give it a try."

Carlos glanced at the full moon. "Right now looks like a good night for it. Well?"

Miguel's aura crackled with feral excitement. "You're on!"

The End

The two novels featuring Roger and Britt, Dark Changeling and Child of Twilight, are now available in a two-book omnibus titled Twilight's Changelings at: http://www.tinyurl.com/TwilightsChangelings

This story mentions another werewolf Britt had treated as a patient. That occurs in Shadow of the Beast, which is currently out of print. Used copies can be found here: https://www.amazon.com/Shadow-Beast-Margaret-L-Carter/dp/189194603X/ref=sr_1_1?keywords=Shadow+of+the+Beast+Carter&qid=1567638030&s=books&sr=1-1

Late Christmas Shopping by Matthew Wilson

Crossing off the list
Brand new stake
To Grandpa Van Helping.

The Black Dog of Newgrange
by
Linda Barrett

Within his darkened apartment room, the tall, thin curly-haired young man named Ian Bledsole lit the candles within the five-pointed star symbol in the center of the filthy room's floor. Sitting prostrate before the pentagram on his sneaker-clad feet, Bledsole intoned:

"Hail Satan prince of darkness and light and the power of the air, I beseech you to take revenge on my American law professor who failed me." The candle's flames reflected off of the lenses of his greasy wire-framed glasses.

Within the pentagram, a ball of fire erupted, dancing before Bledsole's astonished eyes.

"I have helped you thus far," a deep voice roared from within the star-shaped image. "I have aided you in getting on the Dean's list at the Temple University's Dublin campus. You have done well in my service. I shall send you an avenger to take my wrath upon this woman. Look upon him now!" the Prince of Darkness Satan said.

A pitch-black hound leapt from out of the flames. Its red eyes burned within its ebony head. Startled, Bledsole fell backward and the hound pushed its face inches before his nose.

"His name is Barghest! He will obey your every command, including ridding the world of this American, Professor Pamela Brandford." The Unholy One spat out the American's name

"I thank you so much, my L-Lord!" Bledsole revealed his crooked tombstone teeth in a giddy smile.

"If you fail," Satan growled, "he will rip out your heart and your soul."

"There is no way that I will fail you, M-master," Bledsole stammered. "You have the power to exact my revenge on the American!"

Barghest fell before Bledsole in an obedient heap. Bledsole rose upon trembling legs and looked down at the beast.

"Praise be to Satan! Barghest, you have been my answer to my pleas."

****

Under a rainy night, Barghest blended into the darkness. He approached the American professor's apartment in Dublin. His scarlet eyes glowed as he studied the lights in the windows. Taking in the figures inside, he pondered the American woman's face and her husband's. His mastiff's ears listened to their conversation with keen interest. Scarlet eyes studied every inch of their bodies. Pamela was tall and fair with a quiet, reserved manner. Her husband Chuck was brown-haired with horn-rimmed glasses. Barghest needed to make sure he had the right target.

"Pam, are you sure that you'll be all right going to New Grange for the Summer Solstice Ceremony?" Chuck, the American's husband, asked her. "That guy threatened you after you failed him in that class. He's a weird dude!"

Barghest flared his broad scaly nostrils at the husband's description of his master. *How dare he insult his owner?*

"I'm a grown woman," the American said. "I know how to handle myself around him."

"Why don't you have the police escort you up there?" the husband said. "I know a few friends in the FBI and the Garda police who could take you up there and back again."

"It's all right, Chuck. It's in the daytime. What could happen?"

"I'll call someone at the local police department. They'll send up a bodyguard to go with you tomorrow."

"If you insist." Pamela, the American sighed.

Barghest turned and dashed off into the night to where his master awaited. They had to work fast to thwart this action. Pamela must be destroyed in punishment for failing Master Bledsole. His demonic speed propelled him through the forests and through the country roads.

Passing through a forest, he snatched up a hare into his jaws. As he bit his fangs into it, he splattered its blood over a fern's leaves.

Those humans who dared to venture out on such a night as this would take warning at its ebony presence Barghest pondered to himself. *No human agency such as Interpol or the FBI dared to ever challenge Satan's power! Not even God could stand wherever Satan ventured.*

****

Pamela stepped around Newgrange upon the site's wet grass. Last night's rain gave way to the early summer morning's sunshine. She wore her brand-new rubber boots to keep her feet dry.

As she looked around her, it seemed as if the solstice worshipers hadn't shown up yet. She stood alone before the ancient burial mound and an iron statue of a woman from Ireland's Celtic days.

"Good morrow," a soft female voice said behind her.

Pamela turned around to face a slim woman with waist-length black hair and gentle brown eyes. She wore a long cloak over her simple dress. Judging from the clothes the dark-haired woman wore, Pamela thought she could have been a tour guide or a Druid priestess.

"Are you here for the Summer Solstice Ceremony?" Pamela asked.

"Aye," the woman replied. "I have come to guard you against the powers of darkness."

Pamela laughed, not knowing what this person meant.

"It's the summer solstice. I don't know if it's going to be dark for a while. What part of Ireland do you come from?" she asked the woman.

"Not too far from here. Near the Abbey,"

Pamela thought about this.

"The Abbey collapsed in 1644. Oliver Cromwell burnt it to the ground," she reminded the woman. "What's your name?"

"Bridgett. Bridgett of Newgrange," Bridgett said.

"What's your last name?"

"What d'ye mean by that? Newgrange is where I'm from. I live in the Abbey. The one that Bishop Patrick founded a few years ago. Just before he died. And where are you from?"

"America. The United States." Pamela laughed.

Bridgett's thick black brows twisted together on her high forehead.

"America?" she asked.

"Yes." Pamela laughed again. *What is wrong with this woman?* She wondered. *Is she one of these historical reenactors, or is she delusional?* "The United States of America."

"All I know is Ireland. You must be from Britain."

Pamela moved away from Bridgett.

"Are you friends with Ian Bledsole?" Her heart began pounding faster.

"Ian who?" Bridgett asked.

"I have a student who threatened me. I'm a law professor at this university in my home country. Do you know him?"

74

"I know no Ian. Relax." Bridgett held out her hands. "Peace be with you. I mean you no harm." She laughed. "I am a Christian. God will protect you from this evil man. You must look to Him."

"I'll be fine! Stay away from me!" Pamela reached into her fanny pack and pulled out her phone.

Bridgett stood there, blinking her eyes.

"What is that?" she asked.

"Don't joke with me!" Pamela said, pressing her ear to her phone. "Just let me handle this! Chuck," she shouted. "Bring someone up here. I'm being accosted by a deranged woman."

Pulling her cloak's hood over her head, the woman named Bridgett left.

"I'll not disturb you 'til I'm needed," she told Pamela and went up the hill.

Pamela put down her phone and heaved a deep sigh.

"Good riddance to her," she whispered. Pocketing her phone, she made her way towards her car. She should have listened to Chuck's advice.

****

As she opened her car's door, she heard a dog growl. She turned and stared at a black dog with flaming red eyes.

"Hello again," Ian Bledsole said. "Good to see you!" He bared his crooked teeth into a smile which seemed satisfied at her presence. The dog strained at his thick leather leash. Foam dripped from his fangs.

Pamela slipped into the car and locked the door. Bledsole came up to the car and Barghest scratched at the window with his claws.

"I thought you went back to Nebraska after I shamed you in front of all my students!" she hollered through the glass. "I've called my husband, and he's got friends in Interpol and the Garda is coming here in an hour. I suggest you take that dog and hightail it out of here! I've had enough lunatics following me for one day!"

She twisted the ignition and revved the engine. The car was dead.

"You know you shouldn't have failed me." Bledsole wore a triumphant smirk.

She twisted the ignition key again. Nothing worked.

"You plagiarized that paper!" she hollered, inwardly cursing herself and her bad luck.

"It'll take them an hour to get here." Bledsole leaned his hand on the car's door.

Pamela had to think of something. She grasped the steering wheel and reached for her phone. Pressing her thumb on the button, she searched for its power. Didn't she call her husband on this thing a moment ago?

Her body tightened in frustration. The phone's power was also dead.

"I'm waiting for the damn police!" she snarled through gritted teeth.

"By that time, you'll be dead." Bledsole stared down at her with smug eyes.

Pamela stared down at Barghest.

"That dog can't rip through metal and plastic!" she snapped.

"Barghest can do anything. He has the power of Satan behind him," Bledsole said. He quickly unhooked Barghest's leash. The dog leaped onto the car. Pamela jumped into the back seat and reached for her combination snow brush and ice scraper. Barghest snarled as he dove through the car's window. Pamela struck and struck at the beast. Bledsole laughed while he stood there by the car.

"You see," he said in his calm, icy voice. "You can't fight Satan."

"Is that so?" A woman spoke from behind him.

Bledsole turned around to see a woman dressed in Celtic clothes. Her body was covered in a long red cloak. Its hood concealed her face.

"Now I've got a witness to kill!" he muttered. "Barghest! Barghest! Kill!"

Barghest turned away from Pamela. He forgot about the woman's bloody forearms and dove through the windshield for the hooded woman. She tossed back her hood and threw back her cloak. A silver bladed sword shone in her hand. She raised it to Barghest.

Pamela's mouth dropped as the woman whom she identified as the crazy Bridgett held this strange looking sword aloft. Bridgett shouted something. Pamela recognized it as Gaelic. Bridgett's voice echoed through the entire valley.

Lifting his head, Barghest stood still for a moment and then raced towards Bledsole. The great black dog pounced upon the man, digging his claws and fangs into Bledsole's chest. Pamela dove under the back seat. She covered her ears at the stomach-turning sound of her former student's agonized cries.

After a near deafening silence, she heard Bridgett approach the car.

"'Tis over," Bridgett said. "God has protected you once again. St. Patrick sent me to guard and protect you. Good morrow, Pamela Brandford, and may God be with you."

"What?" Pamela asked before passing out from a loss of blood.

****

When she awoke, Pamela found herself being lifted into an ambulance. The Garda members and the paramedics opened their mouths in shock. Tubes ran up and down through her body. A monitor beeped her vital signs. Chuck's mouth drooped in a worried frown.

"Where's the woman?" Pamela asked. "And Bledsole and the dog?"

"What woman and what Bledsole and what dog?" Chuck asked her in gentle tones as he climbed into the ambulance behind her.

"Bledsole was after me," Pamela breathed. "He had this black dog, and he unleashed it onto me."

"Just relax. It's all over," Chuck said.

"What happened?" she asked.

"The paramedics and the Garda found Bledsole dead. His heart was ripped out by some animal. The Garda think that it could have been a wolf who attacked him, but there's no wolves in this area. Are you sure you know what happened? You've been attacked by the same animal. You'd better rest. You've lost a lot of blood."

"But that woman! She saved my life! What happened to her?" Pamela blinked her eyes.

"What woman?" Chuck burst out in tears. "You're hallucinating!"

"She sounded demented. She said God would protect me from Bledsole. She pulled out a sword and killed this animal. This wolf or whatever turned around and attacked him. Where did she go?"

A red-faced female paramedic gradually pushed Pamela back into the stretcher.

"There was no woman. The only one besides you is that statue behind the monument."

"What statue?" Pamela asked as she was injected with a sedative. Her mouth still moved as she dropped off into a long, deep sleep.

A Garda officer gestured to Chuck. He stepped out of the ambulance.

"Your wife's referring to the statue of a saint who lived here at the time of St. Patrick."

"What's this about Saint Patrick? And who's this woman he's talking about?"

The officer pointed to the statue overlooking New Grange.

"Her name was Bridgett. One of his first converts. The Celts killed her because she wouldn't convert to their gods. There's an old legend around these parts."

"What old legend?" Chuck hollered. "My wife was almost killed by one of her students, and you want me to hear about an old legend of a woman murdered by the Celts?"

The officer squinted at him.

"Around these parts, Bridgett saves people in times of mortal danger. Saint Bridgett of New Grange saved your wife's life! From that monster or whatever it was!"

Chuck stared up at the blackened statue. Its metal face smiled down at him.

The End

What Noah Left Behind by Todd Hanks

When Noah built the ark,
he gathered all creatures
of the earth aboard in pairs
just before the Great Flood.

When the rains stopped,
the very first vampire
was standing on the shore
to welcome them home.

Two bats flew off the ark
to perch upon her shoulders.

The Good Samaritan by Matthew Wilson

Never stop for a stranger in the rain
Some lady driver stuck on the roadside
Whose eyes shine bright in lightning
Requesting help from good Samaritans.
It was only a mile to the next town
It was nothing to put her in the car
Until her thanks became a growl
When her smile revealed the fangs.
I was raised a good Catholic boy
Mother's crucifix always around my neck
The creature shrieked when she saw it
Fleeing out into the crashing storm.
Never stop for a stranger in the rain
Things that pass for human in low light
Hungry for the flesh of good Samaritans
Looking to murder lost lady drivers.

Up the Finley Camp Prong
by
Lee Clark Zumpe

Sometimes shadows swarm in the bellies of remote coves and high upon neglected mountain-tops, concealing things so horrible and sinister that should an unlucky soul chance upon it, death would be a most welcome avenue of retreat. No matter the source of these plagues of evil, if left unchecked, their spread is eminent.

Craig had received word only days earlier: Shadows had gathered up the Finley Camp Prong.

Craig drank from a canteen slung over his shoulder as he hiked into the forest. The trail stabbed deep into the backcountry, tracing the course of Cold Springs Creek and gradually climbing Indian Grave Ridge. Earlier in the century, the path served as a railroad bed that carried timber down from the highlands. Relics from those days lay scattered along the way, visible only to the keen observer. New growth obscured most of the remains. The forest had recovered heartily, almost vengefully, seeking to eradicate all vestiges of the past.

Craig finally reached a fork in the stream and headed west, pursuing the Finley Camp Prong towards its source farther up the ridge. The trail worsened immediately as rosebay rhododendron crowded in from all sides. The thick tangle of vegetation affirmed the fact that no hikers had ventured down this road in many years. The Appalachian forest had reclaimed this stretch of land, and it seemed eager not to let it fall into human hands again.

Climbing the steep ridge, Craig paced himself. He moved slowly and gracefully, negotiating each step before his foot touched the ground. He occasionally stopped to refresh himself, to scan the leafy tangle surrounding him and to listen to the forest. After two decades of roaming these mountains, he had learned to understand the voice of the Appalachians hidden in the roar of wild streams and the whisper of wind through stands of American beech.

On this day, the forest urged him to retreat with haste.

Back in the quiet town of Wheeler, Abe Webb served as a living testament to what could become of a man who failed to heed the natural portents of the woods. Sedated, secured by wrist and ankle restraints, he lay unconscious in a bed in an asylum. Even in sleep, visions plagued him. Fits of violent seizures lay claim to him once every few hours, and he would kick and shudder and scream as though enduring harsh physical torture. His eyes would grow wide, his face scarlet red, and he would babble incoherent things as foam gathered on his lips.

Then, as suddenly as the convulsions had begun, he would fall back into a comatose state. Death, the doctors said, was inevitable. Nothing could be done to save Abe Webb.

What had driven this mountain recluse to such a state remained a matter of conjecture. When Abe wandered into Wheeler from the forest a week earlier, naked and raving, locals presumed that his breeding had yielded him a predisposition for madness—but Craig disagreed.

Abe, a legend in many ways, had taken ill while hunting in the woods according to his wife. He and his family lived as far from society as the mountains allowed—in modest cabins set deep in the woods, on parcels of land handed down generation after generation dating back to the time of the pioneers. The mountains of East Tennessee still harbor dozens—some say hundreds—of such families. They go without phones, without electricity, without running water. They farm, they hunt, and they breed, and they want nothing more from life than that.

Abe Wheeler had been such a man. A hillbilly, a backwoods boy, a mountaineer, he had lived more than three-quarters of a century in the wilds of the Appalachians and fathomed more about the mountains than anyone else Craig knew. Abe understood the dark places—he knew that along with the beauty and the resplendence of the wilderness, there was a harrowing and hidden side to its nature. It was Abe who had warned Craig years ago to avoid certain cliffs in certain seasons, to shun a particular ravine and favor a trail when traveling the length of a specific creek. Furthermore, Abe taught Craig about the convergence of shadows beneath secluded promontories and hinted at the things that assembled in the highlands far from the prying eyes of mortals.

Abe had finally succumbed to the swarming shadows, leaving Craig to face them alone. And face them he must, for Abe had warned him often enough of the consequences should such incursions into the world go unchallenged. Though some might consider the hill-jack's farfetched yarns nothing more than senselessness, Craig believed—and he knew he had to act.

A change in the direction of the wind alerted Craig to the passing of a cold front. The treetops swayed uneasily and leaves cascaded down to the forest floor at his feet. Dusk would find him alone in the woods, far from Wheeler and more than a little concerned with his survival. With no more than two hours of daylight left, he knew he would have to pick up his pace to reach the plot of land where once stood a logging camp. There, he would set up camp and spend the night.

He did not expect to get much sleep, though.

****

Craig looked up, watching the thin branches of the surrounding trees quiver as the heat from his campfire rose into the night sky. His dinner churned in his belly, and he drained a flask of whiskey as he waited for exhaustion to overtake him. The remainder of his food—enough for two days— he had neatly packed in his rucksack which was now suspended on a rope ten feet off the ground, tied between two Eastern hemlocks. He did not mind bears smelling his food, but he had no intention of sharing it with them.

He sat amidst the remains of the lumber camp operated by the Finley Company in the first quarter of the century. Signs of its existence could still be found, though the forest had bullied its way back into the patch quite obstinately. Scattered over the grassy forest floor lay bits of coal. A stone wall that had once marked the perimeter of the camp had deteriorated, but a few sections remained intact. Before settling in, Craig had found bits of broken glass and jar lids beneath a red spruce and had guessed that the loggers had furnished themselves with a makeshift still.

He wondered what the men of Finley Camp talked about as they sat around the campfire sampling their moonshine.

Most logging companies remained in operation well into the late 1930s, but the Finley Company abandoned their claims much earlier. By 1922, they had packed up their possessions and were bound for the Northwest, eager to leave the Finley Camp Prong far behind them. No one could blame them after what happened.

In the summer of 1921, logging operations were in full swing along the range. Finley had spent a fortune to set up an infrastructure that could handle the timber coming out of these mountains. He invested in a private railroad and set up a flume on the other side of the crest to handle the red Spruce and Fraser fir. He hired dozens of locals, paying top dollar—in some instances, double what the Little River Lumber Company was shelling out down in the Smokies—and he provided benefits to his employees.

The risk paid off. His loggers cleared twice the expected yield that summer, and productivity continued to grow well into October.

In late fall, things ground to a halt. A carrier out of Wheeler delivering the first lot of winter reserves arrived to find Finley Camp abandoned. Reports claimed that embers in fire rings were still glowing when he walked into the camp, that coffee was still lukewarm in the kettle.

Finley himself visited the camp less than a week later, but no one could find any trace of the loggers. Employees in other camps up and down the range caught wind of the mystery and began to grow restless. Stories circulated, and the old-timers spoke of shadows swarming in the remote reaches of the forest—and of things that gathered during certain phases of the moon.

Craig pulled an amulet from his pocket before retiring to his tent for the balance of the night. The amulet took the form of a stone carved into an eight-rayed star, with a smaller four-rayed star cut on the face of it. Within the smaller star were two concentric circles, and written within these were seven names: Yrmun, Uzaziel, Guraq, Bazyel, Kalaj, Yael, and Ytau'Kharnu. Though to his novice eyes, it appeared to be some kind of ancient relic, Abe had made it for him only a few years earlier. He had been told it was a replica of one that had been handed down in his family for generations. It served as protection against the dwellers in the dark places, and Abe had insisted that Craig never venture into the highlands without it.

Craig had always doubted the charm's effectiveness, but tonight he found himself glad to have it in his possession.

****

A sharp scream split the night and wrenched Craig from sleep. He bolted upright in his tent, tossed aside the unzipped flap of the sleeping bag, and fumbled for his handgun. He felt the amulet dangling around his neck and clutched it instinctively.

Outside, the dull light of his dwindling fire still glowed and cast wavering shadows across the surface of his tent. The night had turned colder than he had anticipated. In the faint gleam which permeated the tent, he could see his breath. He listened intently, still muddled from sleep, trying to determine whether or not the scream had been real or a fruit of his angst-fueled nightmares.

At first, the forest fooled him with silence.

Then he heard them—wailing and moaning piteously, the shrieks of tormented souls filling the night. He listened to a drumbeat thundering throughout the mountains, heard the sounds of whips cracking and guttural voices bellowing out commands. He heard awful cackles and wicked hisses, and he tried to imagine the form of the beasts that could make such hideous noises.

The ill-defined glow from his fire was at once obscured by a more potent crimson light which pulsed from an unknown source. Reluctantly, he unzipped the door of his tent and peered outside, leaning further and further into the night, terrified but intent on seeing the faces of the dwellers in the dark places.

To his horror, Craig found the forest gone. The ridge had been cleared away. Piles of timber stood fifty feet high, waiting to be hauled off for use. The starless night sky had grown cold and gray and ominous. Black-winged things circled overhead, red eyes blazing. Upon the treeless summit of a nearby pinnacle, a tall figure stood before a colossal black gate, directing his minions wordlessly. At his side, a flabby, pallid demon squatted loathsomely. With what appeared to be a human leg bone, this thing struck a large drum at even intervals, setting the pace for the workers below.

Craig focused next on the loggers, and he shuddered at their appearance. Enslaved, they were little more than animated corpses shambling under the watchful gaze of their brutish overseers. Upon each forehead was a brand which took the form of an inverted blood-red pentagram. The slaves' vacant eyes revealed their dismal condition; their scarred pale flesh spoke of the cruel treatment they endured at the hands of their heartless masters. Some fared worse than others. There were mounds of writhing bodies along the old railroad bed, bodies so broken and twisted that their usefulness had been exhausted. Yet death would not, could not claim them. Craig suspected they would spend eternity rotting where they lay.

Though the overseers seemed aware of Craig's presence, they did nothing to keep him from moving about freely outside of his tent. He clutched the amulet Abe had given him, knowing that without it his soul would have fallen prey to these things. Hiking cautiously toward the summit of the mountain, he scouted a position from which he could look through the gate.

The sight he beheld made him stagger backward, trembling and gasping. An empire lay beyond that gate, the scope of which poisoned his mind. Black towers and ebony spires soared into the gray skies of that world, and monstrosities of being flocked within that horrible realm. Yet as vast as it was, he knew instinctively that it could not hope to hold all of its abhorrent breed. The dwellers in the dark places were clearly preparing for war.

Just as Craig's fear had begun to overwhelm him and he sought to escape the scene by any means possible, he chanced upon a familiar face. Relief turned sour when the full meaning of his discovery occurred to him.

"Abe?" he said, staring at the frail-looking figure standing before him. The stench of decay lingered about the man, and his flesh had taken on a bluish hue.

"Craig. You gotta listen to me, boy; ain't got much time."

"Abe ... you're dead?"

"'Course I am, boy; don't reckon I'd stink this bad if'n I weren't, do ya?" He smiled thinly and Craig nodded. Though his spirit went unbroken, his eyes betrayed the infinite pain he suffered. "Now shut your mouth and listen: You've gotta get up to that peak after sun-up and shut this operation down..."

"But, I don't know..."

"Naw, I know ya don't know how, so shut up and I'll tell ya. Ain't nuthin' to it, really. Woulda done it myself if they hadn't found me unprotected—I forgot I gave my dang amulet to 'ya,"

"This is the original?"

"A copy wouldn't do ya no good, would it? I just told ya that to keep ya from blubberin' on me. When I gave ya that, I was sick with the fever if'n ya'll recollect; I didn't reckon I'd make it through that winter. But that don't make no difference now," he whispered. A faint orange ribbon along the ridge heralded the dawn, and the slaves had withdrawn at the bidding of the overseers. "Get up on that peak, find yourself a ring of red trillium. That's all they need to come through from the other side. And all you have to do to seal up the gate again is rip them flowers up outta the ground."

"That's it?"

"Nuthin to it, huh? Just do it, for God's sake ... them boys have gotten too far down the mountain as it is. If we don't put an end to 'em soon, may not be able to stop 'em at all—you hear?"

"Yes ... I understand. I'll make sure that everything is taken care of ... but, what about you?"

"Don't fret none about me, boy. I've got friends on the other side." Abe laughed as he started toward the gate. "We'll abide."

****

The dawn came gradually, almost sluggishly as though some fiendish force conspired to abolish day altogether. But the sun ascended into the morning sky, and with it, the forest on the ridge returned, and the dwellers in the dark places vanished along with all traces of their existence. The morning embraced the mountains as Craig had never seen it do before, like a mother whose ailing child had made a miraculous recovery overnight.

Craig did not linger an instant. He hastily began his climb to the pinnacle where he had seen the black gate, eager to find and destroy the ring of red trillium poor Abe had described. Behind him, Finley Valley welcomed the first light of the day as sunshine poured over the forest of small hardwoods and glimmered on the surface of the creek.

Clambering over loose rocks and exposed roots carelessly, Craig nearly lost his footing on several occasions. Each time, he stopped and reminded himself of the importance of his charge, and that he had many hours of daylight in which to accomplish it. Still, within minutes, his impatience would drown out his caution, and he would be racing headlong up the side of the bluff once more, risking life and limb.

He had almost reached the summit when a flash of white to his left caught his eye. He turned, and gazed down the length of a thin spur trail leading out to what appeared to be a ledge high above the valley floor. Small boulders lay strewn across the flat mantle, most of which was obscured by an outcropping of rock. Something shimmered again, and Craig felt drawn to it.

Rounding the corner, he came upon an unexpected and ghastly sight. There before him, dumped upon the narrow rim of the ridge, lay the skeletal remains of hundreds of people. Their bony frames bleached in the sun, their empty faces pleading for relief. And upon each skull was a brand, a brand that took the form of an inverted blood-red pentagram.

Craig scuffled forward a few steps, horrified by the scene. He needed no investigation to identify these victims. Here were the loggers from the Finley Camp, here were pioneers from the early days of colonization, here were Native Americans whose ancestors so revered these mountains.

But there was more.

Breath seemed to flee from him as he stood swooning, and though he tried to cry out, he found he had no voice. His knees buckled beneath him and he sank to the ground, shivering. Directly before him and encased in writhing veils of maggots and flies were a dozen fresh corpses in various stages of decay. Hikers. Hunters. Forest rangers. Perhaps even citizens from Wheeler. The dwellers in the dark places were adding to their legion of slaves even now.

Remembering the task at hand, Craig stood and began to back away from the field of carcasses. He spun around and sped around rocky outcropping and darted up the slender ribbon of a trail toward the crest of the mountain.

And he slipped.

He fought to right himself, he howled and kicked and clutched at the rocky ground, but it was too late. He tumbled roughly down a steep slope and plunged over the ledge of the ridge ringing Finley Valley. He remained conscious for some time after he had crashed along the bank of the Finley Camp Prong, feeling the cool water wash over his face as it carried the blood away from his wounds. Eventually, darkness came.

He prayed that it was death and not dusk.

****

Craig awoke sometime later, relieved to see sunlight spilling through a nearby window. He found himself clean and bandaged, and lying in a hospital bed. Though his vision was blurred, and his head was throbbing, he rejoiced at the fact he had survived.

His realization that he had lost the use of his legs came almost moments later. His reaction had been violent, drawing the attention of four nurses and two doctors. Only after a considerable amount of sedative had been injected into his bloodstream could the medical staff calm him enough to inform him of his condition.

"Couple of hikers found you," the doctor said flatly, no inflection in his voice, "Up the Finley Camp Prong of all places. That was about a month ago." The doctor jerked his head toward the nurses, and they left the room obediently. He fingered Craig's chart, fastened to a clipboard. "When you got here, you were just barely alive. But you are now expected to recover, although it is not certain that you will ever have full use of your legs again."

Craig nodded lethargically to denote his understanding, then ambled off into a hazy miasma of nightmarish sleep.

He awoke later that evening to hear a woman speaking silently.

"...another one..." she said as she wheeled in a patient. "We'll have to double up this room because the rest of the floor is full. He's got the same symptoms as all the others that have come in since suppertime: Low heart rate, low BP, comatose. It's like an epidemic, but how can these symptoms possibly be contagious. The CDC is flying a specialist in tomorrow morning; we should know more by then."

Craig struggled against the drugs in his system, tilting his head and turning his neck to get a look at his new roommate. As they shifted a young woman from the gurney to the bed, her head tossed limply so that she faced him.

She was branded, but he doubted that anyone else could see it.

Craig could not go back to sleep that night. The sound of a distant drum thundered in his ears, and he shivered uncontrollably as he awaited the arrival of the dwellers in the dark places.

The End

The Gatekeeper's Tower by Marge Simon

A stone structure looms

like a miniature fortress,

beside a dread road,

for it leads to the castle

of a certain pale Count.

Some were given passage,

depending on their mission,

or with an invitation from

the Demon down the road.

The last attendant of the Tower,

performs his duties to this day,

in a disembodied sort of way.

The Snow Globe
by
Todd Hanks

Sam Stedson was a nervous man, an uptight man, a man who liked his underwear to fit a little more than snug, like a jockstrap, and wore a fedora hat that pulled his hair in tight. His pants were short in the legs like he was about to wade through a stream, and he wore the waist of his slacks halfway up to his chest. Around his store were a row of tulips, planted as straight as fence posts. He opened his flea market at seven o'clock sharp every morning of the week, although the nearby stores did not open until ten. Every aisle in the store was labeled: kitchenware, plumbing, tools, books, movies, antiques, yard equipment, etc., and many collectibles were labeled under the vague description of miscellaneous. One item in the aisle marked miscellaneous was a snow globe. The scene inside the glass could have been from a Dickens story, with children in 1800s clothing throwing snowballs in a Victorian city street. Monday's child came into the store at twelve o'clock. She had pigtails and a lollipop.

"Don't get that candy on any of the merchandise!" shouted Sam Stedson. "Where are your parents, anyway?"

"Next door at the shoe store," the little girl replied.

"Well, why don't you go join them?" answered Sam. "If you want to see the store, come back with your parents."

Tuesday's child came in the next day around two o'clock in the afternoon. He had high-topped tennis shoes and a blonde Mohawk. "Where are your parents?" demanded Sam.

"Next door at the shoe store," replied the boy.

"Well, why don't you go and be with them?" said Sam. "I don't like kids in my store without parental supervision."

"But I was going to buy something," said the little boy.

"With what for money?" asked Sam angrily.

"I have my allowance," said Tuesday's child.

"I doubt that," said Sam. "But if you do, you can come back with your parents and spend it."

"No thanks," said Tuesday's child, and exited through the door to the sound of ringing bells. Sam just shrugged.

Wednesday's child came in the next day just before closing time. Sam was in the back and walked up to see the little girl holding the snow globe with the kids inside, throwing snowballs. "Be careful with that," he snapped. "I don't want you to break it. You kids are always breaking something."

Suddenly the air around the little girl swirled. Sam stared in amazement as fog with sparkling green flakes danced around the youngster. Then where Wednesday's child had been stood an ominous figure, an old woman in a black dress with a wide-brimmed dark hat, holding a long wand. "I'm the witch of the inner city," she croaked. "I'm the witch of the bus stop and the vagrants, the back alleys, and the bars. And you are an evil man."

****

A year later, Sam Stedson's younger brother reopened the flea market. He often pondered on the disappearance of his brother. Sam's younger brother was a nice man but known by people to be a bit of a slob. He always wore old jeans and usually had stains on his shirt. His hair was white, wild, and disheveled, a little like pictures of Albert Einstein. But he loved children. There was one item in the store that the new owner did not put back on the shelf to sell. It was the snow globe, with figurines of children inside of it having a snowball fight. The reason the new owner kept this item behind the counter was a figure on the street in front of the children, a man in slacks pulled up to the middle of his chest and a tight-fitting fedora, a person who looked so much like his older brother.

The End

Haiku by Denny E. Marshall

misses her so much
he had to see her again
grabs worn out shovel

arrive at hell's door
so full told come back later
unsure of next move

duct tape around mouth
roll covers nose by mistake
no ransom call made

witch cast magic spell
now in monopoly game
didn't see the train

enjoy wife's garden
think the plants are beautiful
wish they wouldn't bite

Shadow Sheila and her Abettor
by
Rajeev Bhargava

"Let me out of here! Let me out! I'm not crazy. Can anyone hear me?" She cried out, scratching at the thick padded walls of her isolated cell.

The agitated voice belonged to a frail, young lady, aged twenty-two. Her real name remained anonymous since the first day when she was captured by staff last winter, running in the untamed woodlands that surrounded the centuries-old building aptly named *Mystic Woods Mental Institution*. Apparently, they believed she was a lycanthrope as they caught her, using a net, licking a blood-soaked human skull. Where she found it, only she knew, and she wouldn't tell.

Over the years of her imprisoned confinement, she had been kept away in a pitch-black, soundproof cell, isolated from other patients due to her strange habit of claiming to communicate with ghostly apparitions that moved around on the walls. This had a negative, disturbing impact on everyone, including the other patients who would cover their faces and hold their ears, pacing up and down, some crouching on the floor as she screamed and roared like a wolf. This was brought to the attention of the head of the institute, a dignified elderly man of ninety-seven, named Dr. Hans Ghoulder who ordered her transfer to solitary confinement in the "deepest and darkest corner room" immediately. He warned all staff to enter her cell in pairs at all times.

Still frantic, she stormed to one corner of her room and fell on the cold floor, barefoot, then began sobbing. She yelled and tore at her already tattered rag dress. But now, as she was seemingly forgotten and out of sight, nobody noticed or cared. She stood up again abruptly, then pounced to the door.

Sheila "X" then stretched out her hands like a she-wolf and growled, after which she scratched and clawed at the padding of the entrance door. So much so, that her nails filled with blood and left impressions of her fists on the material. Her fists clenched, and she began to hem with all her might, but it was no use. The padding was very thick, which made it soundproof. She then flexed and curved her hands.

"Hooowwl! Hooowwl! This is one angry she-wolf." She growled in a violent frenzy and then scratched the cloth with such force that her already bitten nails filled with streaks of blood, which oozed from her nerves. In frustration, she spat at the door, then returned to the back right corner of her cell and cupped her face, crying.

"You'll be sorry for what you did to me, you heartless monsters! Sob … sob. I know you can all hear me; you're just pretending you can't…" Her pained voice faded to pin drop silence.

Just then, a brilliant red glow appeared and filled the entirety of the right-side wall.

"What's happening!? G… get away from me!"

Instead, before her eyes, it formed into a slender and sleek shape and shadow of a female figure, who sat cross-legged.

Her fear turned to fascination, and she walked up to it and stared hard. When she reached out to touch it, the shadow glided to a far side of the wall, as if frightened, then up to the ceiling.

"Hey! I thought *I* was the frightened one."

She sat on the floor, cross-legged, and placed her hands on her cheeks, indicating boredom.

"I don't know why you ran away from me. I mean, I can't harm you. I just want someone to talk to … a friend. You see, I'm … lonely. I … don't even know what time of the day or night it is."

The shadow, then sat cross-legged and placed its hands against its head, leaning forward as if listening.

"Welcome to Hell. Seeing we're both sharing the same cell, how about us becoming real friends?" She extended her right hand. "Oh, but wait, I haven't even given you a name yet. Now let me see…"

She thought hard and then snapped her fingers and said, "It can only be Shadow Sheila!"

Just then, the main door burst open, and two staff, a sharp-faced man in his mid-twenties known as Meroni Stenson, and a short-haired lady in her mid-forties called Erica Bezotta entered her cell.

"Careful, Stenson," said Bezotta, wide-eyed.

"Yeah." He froze upon seeing the frail figure and her surroundings, then felt sick to his gut at the sight of the blood around her face. Bezotta grabbed a plate with a loaf of bread and a bowl of soup from his hands and quickly placed it on the floor, not losing eye contact with Sheila "X."

"I don't want yours or anybody's pity. I just want out of here!"

This time, even Bezotta shook. Both assistants retreated and reached for the cell door. At that instant, an eerie cracking sound broke the silence. The door slammed shut behind them, followed by a bolt that confirmed it was locked, which left them all in the darkness.

"Please, somebody open the door!" cried Stenson. "We're trapped inside!"

"Now you see how it feels? To be trapped inside a cell … with a she-wolf. Ha ha ha ha haa! Now, we can have some real fun, all night long, hah hah hah hah hah! Aaah-ooooooooooooooooh!"

"Listen, I don't know what game you're playing, Sheila 'X,' but this could have serious consequences, so you better let us out of here," said Bezotta. She dug into her left side pocket and illuminated the room with a lighter.

After she lit it, a pair of arms snaked down through the ceiling and pulled Stenson upwards, throttling him until his body went limp. The body dropped, then roasted and drizzled until it turned into a heap of cinders on the floor, then faded into oblivion. No trace of Stenson remained; it was as though he'd never existed. Sheila "X" looked upwards and grinned, then turned to Bezotta and gave a menacing snarl. Her eyebrows had thickened and merged in the middle. Furthermore, she now appeared taller as she stalked Bezotta around the cell menacingly.

"Keep away from me. Keep away or I'll…" In the next instant, Sheila "X" pounced upon her, forcing Bezotta to drop her lighter. This was followed by loud screams and the tearing of flesh.

Moments later, Bezotta's corpse lay on the blood-stained cell floor, after which, Sheila "X" gazed up at the ceiling and whispered, "Thank you, Shadow Sheila. I feel a lot safer now, with you."

There was no reply, no glow this time.

"I guess you must be sleepy." Sheila "X" yawned. "I think I'm going to turn in myself. But boy, am I hungry." In reply, a plate of salad, sandwiches, and fresh fruit appeared through the wall before her on a golden tray. Her eyes lit up.

"Wow! Where were you all this time? Now, I can kiss hunger goodbye! Thank you, Shadow Sheila."

As she took a bite, a thought entered her mind that maybe she could ask Shadow Sheila to help her to escape, but only once she got to know her a little better. She yawned again, then curled up on the cold floor. Her eyes grew heavy, and before long, she drifted into a deep sleep.

90

The following day, in the midafternoon, she awoke to find herself lying on a long table. She was wearing a helmet and had on a straightjacket, her limbs tied, with electrodes protruding at her feet.

A small team of nurses headed by Dr. Ghoulder surrounded her. He approached her and asked in a dry, croaky monotonous voice, "Has anybody seen Stenson and Bezotta?"

No response.

Dr. Ghoulder glanced at an assistant who stood by a machine.

"Give her a small shock." The assistant, a young man named Yang Choo, reached for the voltage switch and pressed.

"Aaahhhh!!!" His body ignited and burst into white-hot flames.

"Quick, someone put the fire out!" shouted Dr. Ghoulder. But the moment he said it, everyone froze until a heap of ashes lay on the floor where Yang Choo had stood. The ashes faded into nothingness, after which, everyone found themselves able to move again. They turned to one another, wide-eyed and confused.

Dr. Ghoulder gazed at the empty space where the assistant had stood, then glared at the inpatient furiously.

"You're responsible for this. I … I was wrong about you all along. I thought you were just another mentally ill patient, suffering from lycanthrope, but now, I realize you're some kind of a sorceress."

"Well, then you had better release me right away, or else, you'll all share the same fate."

"Are you actually *threatening me!?*"

"No, I'm *warning you!*"

"Well, suppose I say you're bluffing? You know, I've never lost a poker game." His attention turned to the voltage machine, and he reached for the button.

"If you value your life, don't do it."

Dr. Ghoulder marched to the button and pressed it.

The electricity zapped through her body, causing her to writhe, screaming until smoke sizzled through her hair, palms, foot soles, mouth, and ears. Seconds later, she blacked out.

When she awoke, she found herself back inside her cell, in the darkness. Her body was still hurting and her eyes burned. She placed her hands across them and felt swollen rings around them, due to the shock. Then, she recollected her thoughts and shouted out in the darkness:

"Hey! You betrayed me in my hour of need. What were you thinking!? I thought you were my friend, Shadow Sheila!"

In response, something cracked, reminiscent of an object that had fallen from a great height. As she couldn't see anything, she felt the floor around her, until…

"Ewww. There's something wet lying here," she said to herself, feeling it. She brought it closer to her face and inhaled.

"Oh no, it's a decapitated human head!" At first, she instinctively tossed it to the ground, grimacing. But her repulsion shortly changed to an eerie interest. Once again, she lifted the head and decided to take a bite. Her teeth sank into the flesh of its cheekbone, and she took a deep bite.

Just then, the door opened, and Dr. Ghoulder stood facing her.

"Choo's dead. You killer, I'm going to teach you a les…" His words drowned to a whisper and were cut short by the horrific scene before him.

There she sat, holding a human skull, soaked in blood, stripping off pieces of flesh and chewing them.

"Mmm, this is delicious. Want to try some, Ghouli?"

Ghoulder's face paled at the sight, and he fought back the urge to vomit. He then produced a syringe from his left coat pocket. To her surprise, he injected it into his forehead and laughed harshly.

"I know what you're thinking, Sheila Ashvernser, and no, you're not hallucinating; far from it."

"But … how did you know my name!"

"Oh, I've known all along. I'm psychic."

"Psycho is more like it," she muttered. "I hate to ask, but I'm just curious to know, why on earth would the head of a psychiatric institute stab his forehead, of all places, and with a syringe!?"

"Why would a young lady claiming she's not lost her sanity drink human blood and tear off flesh from skulls?"

She shrugged, then tossed the skull to the floor and wiped the blood from her lips, spitting out the flesh, some of which had wedged in her teeth.

"Never mind. I'm not interested, nor do I care, because now I'm going to reveal to you who I am, and more importantly, who *she* is."

Before she could respond, he stared up at the ceiling and pursed his lips, then produced a high-pitched shriek.

In an instant, Shadow Sheila dropped to the floor for the first time, standing between them.

It didn't end there. Dr. Ghoulder's appearance changed, as well. First, his clothes dissolved from his body. At first, he appeared stark naked, but then something strange occurred.

He began to metamorphosize. Orange scales emerged through his flesh, all over his body. His tongue split into two, and he hissed. His eyeballs turned a fiery red.

"The clue was in my name, you seeee … hssssss."

When he spoke, smoke seeped from his mouth.

"Let me explain … hssssss"

Her eyes filled with terror and she gazed longingly toward the door,

But Shadow Sheila had now moved there.

"And here's the part you're really gonna relish, Ashvernser. Your friend and I have known each other for eons … since childhood, in *Hell*. Hah hah hah hah hah!"

"No, this is not happening!"

In desperation, she made a dash for the exit, only to find her body set ablaze. She burned into a heap of white-hot ashes, which disintegrated into nothingness…

The End

The Doleful Tale of the Bucket of Blood
by
Francis-Marie de Châtillon

Part I

It's A.D. 1722 and a freezing winter's night sometime in early January. Snow blankets the ground and hugs at the trees. A man is writing nervously in his journal. His handwriting, usually so well crafted, is faltering now and betrays the porter and brandy he has been overconsuming in the last days; but not only this, for the weeks before Christmas and St. Stephen's he had passed in wakeful fear both for his life and his sanity. Even a casual observer can see that his eyes stare crazed-like from the library into the grounds of his capacious country house. Suddenly, a loud crack and spit from the fire see him jump in alarm. He looks sharply around the room and its many beautiful volumes. A long woeful moan escapes him, and he buries his face in his hands, displacing backward his fashionable wig. He takes up the quill again and continues writing…

The True and Unvarnished Journal of:
Sir Humphry Valentine Cuthbert Hynde, Bart.
of Upper Threshing, Berkshire.

To those who come upon this poor journal, I must ask their forbearance in the reading of and, indeed, their forgiveness for its shameful content. Oh, for in truth this is a record of proceedings most contrary to God and man. I pray for mercy for my part in those events; yet I expect no clemency. That said, read on, and of your charity offer the highest petition for my miserable soul.

Our gracious king, George of Hanover, had been enthroned but seven years when my downfall started. It was during the Christmas period, and Epiphany had not yet come. The weather was bitterly cold with much wind; yet my heart was happy and lifted. The early season's round of parties had been successful, and many *alliances romantiques* had been formed. High in spirits and looking for more entertainment, I had written and sent posthaste to my oldest friend, Lord Willoughby in Kent. I suggested we should travel together down to the West Country, where my aunt, Lady Frances Somerville, was entertaining at her estate for the New Year period. Despite the inclemency of the weather, I envisioned little problem with the journey as the turnpikes were usually negotiable, and we would take extra horses and servants in a second coach to assist us if we became stuck.

So it was that I waited that fateful Friday after Christmas for Jasper to arrive. We had planned to spend the Saturday here at Threshing Court near the Berkshire-Wiltshire border, and leave Sunday so as to have plenty of time for our arrival by New Year's Day on the Thursday. Although but two, I had my cooks prepare a lavish table for the evening meal I was anticipating: winter soup, cod and oyster sauce, fowl *la Montmorenci*, glazed ham, lamb chops, and various delights of goose, pies and tarts, beefsteak *chateaubriand*, quails, and many buttered vegetables and jellies.

I waited quite impatiently, but only because I hadn't seen Willoughby for many months now. He had been invited to the same social events, the same round of parties, but we had not always been mutually available to attend. So my impatience was born out of a quiet excitement. Willoughby, like me, was approaching 30. Like me, he was extremely wealthy. Like me, a keen swordsman in and out of the bedchamber. He was taller than me, with a more aesthetic look to his cast.

I watched from the great dining room window up the long tree-lined drive as the afternoon light began to fade, hoping there had been no issue to detain Willoughby. Then, standing by the fire,

I poured myself a stiff brandy and downed it in a single draught, then poured another. I had just thrown myself into a large chair, pondering some nebulous problem when I thought I could hear the clatter of hooves approaching; going to the window, I saw in the distance the laboring of horses and a coach approaching at a steady trot. "Hoskins!" I shouted. Hoskins was my personal manservant and a trusted fellow. He entered quickly, for he was a fellow who could anticipate my needs in most circumstances, and in all probability had also been watching out. "Hoskins man, move the servants into action quickly! See that Lord Willoughby is well received from his coach!" With that, Hoskins left me at a brisk march to attend my greeting, and organize the billeting and feeding of Willoughby's servants and stowage of all the accompanying impedimenta.

It was not long before I greeted Willoughby in the library after he had divested of his traveling garments.

"Hynde! My dear fellow! Give me a drink, I'm parched and cold!" he cried as he entered. Willoughby was known as a straight-talking type and I admired him for it.

"With the greatest of pleasure, Jasper!" I said, as we clasped hands firmly and embraced in the manly fashion of the English.

I poured Willoughby a large cup, and we drank our mutual health in goodly measure. We warmed by the bright fire clutching our mulled wine and fortifying ourselves further with the small winter game-pies, which are traditional in this part of Berkshire. We talked: Willoughby was making damnation of the bitter journey and the many frustrations at his estate; I the reluctant flogging I'd administered to some recidivist in the village, along with more merry banter. Soon, however, Willoughby said,

"You know, the weather here is worse than in Kent, and I've heard tell that it may be worse in the West of the country. So we should leave Upper Threshing pretty early on the morrow, don't you think, Hynde?"

"To that, Willoughby, I've already given instructions. We shall be ready to go immediately after our breakfast, which will be taken earlier than usual at 8:00 a.m., if that suits."

"It's a capital plan, Hynde." Then *sotto voce*, "The turnpikes are good, Humphry my friend, but they may be unreliable." He was looking a little pensive and I cocked an eye at Willoughby, as he was unknown to pessimism.

Oh! I wonder now, as I scratch on these pages, did he have any six-sense inkling of the mournful happenings that would soon overtake us? I remember casting my gaze to the darkening afternoon and the sudden snow flurries that sped topsy-turvy past the windows, and I felt a pale hand of something unknown pass over our expected merriment.

Part II

These uneasy feelings soon evaporated as dinner approached. Willoughby had always made a good plate; it amazed me how he could eat and drink so much without putting on even a grain of *avoirdupois*: I, in contradistinction, went to fat. Our jolly dinner was made finer, as it happed, by the unexpected arrival of Sir Sidney Spencer, my nearest neighbor. He called to present me with the compliments of the season, which he had not been able to do due to circumstances, and with this a handsome gift of a rundlet of aged brandy. I invited him to stay and dine. Now, Sir Sidney was a game fellow in his early 60s. He had that florid complexion of a true pleasure seeker and a girth to match. Being the King's commissioner for wheat in the counties of Berkshire and Wiltshire, and making the most of the opportunities the position afforded, he had consequently become rich beyond his humble boyhood expectations.

Dinner was announced at 8:00 p.m. We sat in fine form, relaxed and free from the strictures of protocol that attach themselves to dining when ladies are present. My dogs all lay about awaiting the predictable fun, which they knew from of old. There were the expected jokes, the inevitable innuendo concerning a certain elderly Lady M (at which Sir Sidney seemed to laugh too heartily, too hastily, not have seeded that particular furrow), and much more nonsense besides. The fire in the dining room burned briskly with only the occasional blow-back of smoke due to the strong winds that had developed over the afternoon and evening. Yet the sudden loud chattering of the windows as a blast hit them, and the ghostly scratch-scratching of the ivy and overhanging branches of a tree against them gave me again disquiet.

"I say, Sir Humphry, you always have a fine table. Fine table indeed, young man!" he remarked loudly, and with that (and it was one of the sports we gentlemen enjoy when dining), he put down 24 silver shillings. "I put it on that deer-hound of yours, Hynde, at 3-1. There!" Willoughby slammed down his silver and picked my otter-hound, and I, in turn mine, on a small ratting terrier I kept in the house. We each picked a couple handfuls of goose bones and fowl parts and flung them across the room. With whoops, we excited the dogs to the game.

The dogs, for their part, seeing the fun now afoot, shot forward and raced each other for the pieces. The winner was the dog that gained the bones first and devoured them the fastest. It was a mêlée of fun, barks, snaps, and snarls! We jumped up and down, banging on the table, at the antics of the canines. Then again, more flesh and bones flew around, for the first was only to prime the dog's excitement and to spur them. I saw the otter-hound, keen as mustard, dive under a Doberman and snatch a duck's leg away from a Flat-Coated Retriever. The retriever then chased elsewhere and jumped on a plover carcass that was overlooked somehow. Yes, a real mêlée! Who had the upper hand was still in the balance. I was still confident of my little ratter when the wine of our enjoyment turned as bitter as the bitterest gall.

Malmsey, one of my red-setters, as sweet a bitch as you could imagine and named after that famous sweet Mediterranean wine, was savagely set on by the otter-hound. The other dogs, hearing the attack, their blood up in competition and obeying their natures, turned their attention to her. It was fast and furious. She screamed in fear and pain as teeth tore into her. She tried to run headlong to me but was gripped by a hind leg. In complete submission, she tried to roll and show her belly, as dogs and wolves do; but the others had, as I say, truly their blood up. The huge deer-hound ripped her open in one ghastly, grisly, and sanguineous shake. We, horror-stricken yet fearing intervention, had made only small ground towards the impending carnage that would be Malmsey. I saw the deer-hound eye us predatorily, head down and walking slowly towards us, preparing an imminent attack. The look made my blood run cold. Quickly, I pulled my pistol and shot it dead. It fell near to what was the husk of Malmsey. Servants were now banging hard on the door, shouting because of the noise and the pistol-shot. Spenser flung the door open to them, and to a man, they stood agape at the scene.

Later, the dinner cold in our stomachs and spirits, and the servants whipping the frenzied dogs out into the icy night, we sat at the table again. Willoughby was the first to speak, "Damnable thing, Hynde. Damnable thing that!" He gripped my arm. We drank some more, and then more to assuage our unpleasant feeling. I brushed it all off as absolutely of no consequence. I lied. The silence was thick as Spencer pushed the 24 silver shillings to me. He muttered something inaudible and then called Hoskins for his cloak. He said nothing more to me before he left. Perhaps he felt some guilt, but I cannot say. As I write of this unhappy ending to a convivial evening, I ask you, could there have been any clearer auger of doom to come?

Part III

The events of the previous evening were now calmer in our minds and with the restorative of sleep, Willoughby and I left full-hampered for the West Country that Sunday morning. We decided not to have breakfast but to get on. The weather was turning in on us, and we had to make it to the inn of the *Traveler's Respite* at the end of the second turnpike, which was just over the Wiltshire-Somerset boarder. This was a good distance. Hoskins was with us, sitting on top with my coachman, all wrapped against the biting cold and the increasing snowfall. The second coach, with burly servants (for protection and muscle if we got stuck) and four trailing horses, followed close behind. We passed reasonably soon from the familiar parts of Berkshire with its mixture of pasture and woodland, which gave way to more thickly forested parts of Wiltshire. Willoughby and I passed the brandy flask to and fro for nips to ward off the cold: it seemed that even the inside of the coach had become an ice house. I looked from the coach windows at the steep, snow-covered hills dotted with ancient trees; odd stony outcrops of rock came into view that seemed to have been crafted by an unknown race. Trees, hung with increasing snow, became giant ghosts of childhood fears, and in the dimness of rising twilight, shadows played tricks and the imagination fed on them.

Coach journeys are long, bumpy, and rough on one's frame, and need considerable preparation. Signs are unreliable: they fall over or twist in the wind; milestones can be worn to illegibility; landmarks obscured in lousy weather. Towards evening, some miles into Wiltshire and anticipating our inn late that night, a tremendous thud hit the top of the coach, and Willoughby and I jumped with fright. I thought a bough had come down on us and caused damage. I banged hard with my cane on the coach roof and shouted a halt.

"What the devil was that, Hoskins? Are you alive? Dead? What?" I pulled the window down sharply and put my head out into the freezing night.

"All 'twas but a block of ice, Sir 'umphrey. Fell off a tree. Though fair near did for the coachman, sir!" He sniggered at the thought, and it angered me. He could be a little immature.

"Then, be careful, man!" I cried back. "Lord Willoughby and I cannot be left here with a dead coachman. Understand?"

"Sir 'umphrey."

With us fully apprehensive, the journey wore on, and proper darkness engulfed us. Progress lessened considerably as the snow had become a blizzard. The brandy flask passed between us repeatedly; hampered food also. How I wanted to cry out for hot beefsteak or a hot lamb pot! The road, already churned in previous weeks by rain, was now frozen and littered with ice. I began to regret the unwisdom of my plans to visit my aunt in such weather. It was a little later that Willoughby had an idea, one we should have seen well before. The following coach had four men inside and that coach was followed by four horses. Should we not use them as outriders? They could carry torches and show the way! This sounded like a capital idea, and soon we were moving again, but still slower than earlier. After a half-hour, we encountered a sign post, which should have directed us to the route we needed. But to our dismay, it stood at an angle with the directions pointing to the ground or the sky. This only enhanced my growing alarm. We took what seemed to be the broader road, reasoning it to be a "pike" road and so lead us to our destination. Soon, we entered a thick piece of forest where the road just wound on, and disconcertingly the wood thickened still further. It seemed to envelop us as the branches reached ever lower and skitted over us. Worse, in the flicker of the torches, I thought I saw some hideous creature, something demonic stalking us tree-to-tree, seemingly waiting with some gruesome design. I shuddered inside my traveling clothes and held my breath. Then, a loud cry was let out by one of the outriders, and to my further dismay, we discovered the second coach had hit a particularly deep rut and thrown a wheel and, slithering sideways into a ditch, had then broken the back axel!

We were now in the worst of all possible pickles. The coach was stuck fast and, in the tip, had shed our baggage into the snow. Luckily, we freed the horses and tethered them to mine and Willoughby's coach. After much debate, Willoughby and I decided that we should go on with Hoskins as our outrider. The others could wait with the stranded transport until we could reach the inn and seek some assistance. Reluctantly, we moved on, and I have to confess I feared for those left behind as my mind played over the "thing" my fancy had seen.

Luck was not on our side. After some time and very late of clock, Hoskins reported a tree down across our path. Coated with heavy ice and fresh snow, the tree had succumbed to gravity and blocked our way. Willoughby and I stared at each other and drank deeply from the flask. Unable to turn around (for what purpose I know not, as the other coach blocked any way back), we could only go forward. Again, we released the two draw-horses and tethered them on long ropes. Hoskins was detailed to stay with the coach whilst Willoughby and I went ahead on foot. Hoskins was to return to the other coach, and all were then to ride back and report events if he failed to receive help here by daybreak.

Willoughby and I walked on for a seeming eternity when we perceived a dim light in the thickness of the woods. Our hearts leapt. We crashed through the undergrowth and low-hanging branches, receiving small cuts and bruises and tears to our attire. Willoughby stumbled many times in the entanglements of brambles; I careered and fell over an unseen log. It was as if the forest was our bitter enemy. On gaining the light source, we were staggered to see that it came from a window of a small inn well hidden among the trees. A fire flamed in what was the taproom for the common sort. No name hung to distinguish the inn—but we cared little for that—and finding the door, knocked hard for entry.

Part IV

Our insistent demands with the knocker and hanging-bell were eventually answered in the form of a middle-aged, stout man whom one could reasonably surmise was the innkeeper. Through the door, we could see that it presented as clean and well ordered, with a background smell of ale and food. We thanked God! The innkeeper spoke first.

"Good gentlemen, how may I help you this night if I can?" He eyed our disheveled and muddy state with some interest.

"His Lordship and I are traveling down to Somerset. My aunt, Lady Somerville, is expecting us; shortly back on route, our coaches came adrift. We will spend the night and pay," I said, in the usual manner of these simple dealings. "Bring food and drink. You will also need to get assistance to our servants and horses stranded some way back."

Willoughby made to enter; yet the keeper seemed hesitant, as he made no customary welcome nor acknowledgment of our rank, and did not remove himself from the door frame. Then:

"Good sirs all, it would be impossible to help you now as all the inn is asleep and closed tight for the night. Is there no other...." His voice trailed off questioningly.

"Absurd man, I am Lord Willoughby of Lamberhurst, cousin to the Marquis of Maidstone. Here before you also is Sir Humphry Hynde of Upper Threshing, Berkshire. A magistrate. Now move aside and victual us. And clean beds, mark you!"

At this, the man's demeanor changed to one of the most obsequious and helpful, and he moved aside with the speed of a prize-fighter. We entered into a warm, tolerably furnished room, threw off our traveling cloaks, and sat near the fire warming ourselves. The inn-keep speedily brought ale, wine, and brandy and then started to roll out all manner of hot food: a large piece of roast beef appeared, a crown roast of mutton, roasted potatoes and turnips, and butter and bread. We fell on it like famished winter wolves.

"I'll make the arrangements for your retinue, good sirs. Will they require rooms here? In the loft?"

"They will. See that the horses are stabled and foddered also," I answered. He bowed low and scuttled off about his duties, leaving Willoughby and me to eat and drink like men just saved from a circle of Hell.

It was sometime later, after we had devoured the food and were calling for more brandy, that a young buxom girl came to clear the table. She was pretty, with tousled blond hair and a fine smile. I could see that she had caught Willoughby's eye in a moment, as he was watching her every move. A few minutes later, after more observation, he beckoned her.

"Young girl, forgive me but I forgot to ask the keep here the name of this happy inn, pray tell it me." His voice was soft yet commanding and I hazard I knew his intentions.

"Why, sirs, this is *The Lamb* and finer name for a house that has saved many a soul there isn't." Her voice was enticing. She smiled at us and I could see Willoughby fairly warming, and not from the fire.

She brought more brandy, and some while later the inn-keep arrived, bringing us news that our servants and horses were safe and our baggage recovered. Capital news! The inn-keep stood waiting for further instructions, I imagine, for he made no bow or move to retire from us. I was watching Willoughby closely in a sideways fashion, for a change had fallen over him. He seemed to have the cast of a driven man; an intensity in his eyes that was strange and unexpected.

"Good inn-keep, the girl that latterly served us; I desire a warm bed this night so have her sent to me soon as I retire. Make sure she's clean and presented well. She will be treated kindly and I will pay."

To this, the innkeeper stared back, at first blankly, and then with a sort of pleading dismay and alarm. He became animated to the highest degree. "Oh, my Lord, my Lord, so great a man as yourself sir, would be but poor served by such a one! She's young—why she just turned twenty, look you—and not yet versed in the ways of the bedchamber and the pleasing in thereof!" He was truly perturbed, yet I could not hazard why. I was curious.

Willoughby cried, "What is it to you? I said I would pay and *that* should be your only concern! Absurd man, you will do as I tell you." He followed this in a low voice that had every menace. "I will take no refusal in this matter!"

Now, the keep threw himself to his knees before us, his hands high as in Christian supplication before the Cross, and with tearful eyes, he pleaded, "Good Lordship, she is my daughter, my only daughter! Have compassion! I beg you take another. I have ... I have a girl in the kitchen that will be biddable to be put to it. Or, my Lord, even my wife! Good sir, take her for your enjoyment; she be eleven years younger than me, my Lord, and she has life in the bedchamber!"

"Curse you, man. The French pox on your wife. I don't want your *wife!* What ails your thinking? I want that girl and have her I will. Mark it!" I took Willoughby gently by the arm at this to steady him in his unusual outburst.

"My lord, I will not do it. I can't." He said this flatly with his tears falling to the wooden floor. I felt a little sorry for him.

"Can't? *Can't?* Or is it *won't?* You dog!" Before I could hold Willoughby further, he was up from his chair and had hard cuffed the inn-keep across the face. The poor man fell sideways from his knees, crashed into a drinking stool, and rolled prostrate. Willoughby then drew his sword, moved forward, and was about to make light work of him when I, now also on my feet, grabbed Willoughby's arm.

"Hold up! Hold up! Willoughby, this is madness. Madness! For a wench? Forcing a girl is one thing for us of rank, but *murder*? Murder will surely follow us like a dog smelling like a bitch in heat! Think man!" I pleaded hard with him, and after a moment or two, I saw the anger drain from his eyes. Willoughby, thankfully for us, put away his sword. He sank back into his chair and took a large swallow from the brandy bottle. I asked the innkeeper if our rooms were ready and he nodded slowly. A large grazed cheek presented itself, along with a fast-forming bruise.

I helped Willoughby up the two flights of stairs to the "gentle rooms." I was accommodated at the far end of the hallway, and Willoughby, strangely I thought, at the end nearest the stairs, there being four rooms between us. Fires burned in each room. The beds looked clean and well aired. Blankets were provided, and all had the feeling of giving a comfortable night, despite the sparsity of carpet. As we knew not about our baggage or servants, apart from being recovered, I helped Willoughby lay in his clothes on the bed and then covered my poor friend with a blanket or two. Satisfied that he was comfortable and hearing the first breaths that denote the onset of slumber, I was content to leave him for the night and retire to my own room, and there, hopefully, sleep. Once there, I threw another log on my fire, and likewise, fully clothed, lay upon my bed. The inn was quiet—too quiet, I fancied, for I heard no moaning or snoring from any of the rooms. Sleep came quite soon. As I write this, you, poor reader, will realize that I omitted my prayers for the night, and this unhappy omission was a mistake concerning the events that I now relate.

Part V

How long I slept I do not know. My pocket watch, always a reliable timepiece, had stopped at midnight; it must have been the fall in the forest just before we gained the inn that had caused it so. I lay in the flickering light of the fire, thinking how close we had come to disaster on the journey. It wasn't much after these thoughts had passed, and as I again drifted off into soft-slumber, that I thought I heard footsteps on our landing. They were light in touch but nonetheless clearly discernible. They were approaching my door but then stopped, turned, and padded back, stopping further down. I wondered if another guest had left their bed, but I was sure we were the only occupiers on this landing. I harkened harder, and heard the turn of a knob then the slow creak of a door. Swiftly, I left my bed and put my ear to the door. The sounds were coming from near the stairs, and so to be at Willoughby's room or thereabouts. I gently opened my door a crack to better hear what followed, if anything. For a few moments, there was no sound at all, but then I heard, "Ahhh. You've come." It was Willoughby's voice without doubt, aristocratic and crisp even in sleepiness. I laughed under my breath. The dog had gotten his bone after all, and I marveled at whether the inn-keep, so guarded of his daughter's virtue, knew she had tiptoed up to give the honey from her hive. Ha! Such a jape indeed. I closed the door again and then lay back on the bed.

I was drifting nicely back into restfulness when the most appalling shrieks and screams occurred. I heard things crashing to the floor. The sound of smashing mirrors. The door banging back and forth with shocking force. Incoherent cries for help rang through the air, and God knows what else. My blood ran ice-cold as I knew the voice seeking help to be not that of a girl—but of Willoughby's! Jumping up, I ran, bootless, to where the chaos emitted, which was, as I thought, my friend's room. The door was shut, and upon trying the knob, I found it fast locked against me.

"Willoughby! Willoughby man! Open the door! What's happening?" I cried aloud for help, but nothing stirred in the inn. The noise from within Willoughby's room was almost deafening. I charged the door with my shoulder, but despite its seeming ordinariness as doors go, it was as solid as a tree!

"Willoughby!" I shouted through the door. In return, the door thumped hard at me and seemed to bow in and out. "Ye Gods, what's going on?" I screamed.

Running back to my room, I took my flintlock and sword and ran back to Willoughby's accommodation. As I gained the door, to my immense surprise, I saw the figure of the blonde serving wench from earlier just disappearing down the stairs. I was transfixed. She was wearing a white night shift and carrying a well-bucket from which hung, limp-like, something over the side. I thought to fire at her, but was more concerned for my friend. Finding that the door now admitted me with ease, I entered the room.

What scene lay before me I find hard to relate to you in this journal. Words, which usually do not run from me, seem far on the horizon of my speech. Willoughby lay prone on his bed, his clothes ripped to tatters, as if attacked by a wolf; yet he bore no sign of injury. His breathing was stertorous. His face was deathly white, and his wide eyes stared horrified as if having encountered the very Devil himself. Yet he lived! The room was in total disarray, but this is a mean word to describe the pandemonium I encountered. Things were smashed everywhere. A candlestick of brass was driven into the stone of the wall. The fire itself was cold and lay upended around the room, its soot and debris all over. Blankets were ripped and strewn all around; pillow feathers also. My God, what a sight!

After seeing to Willoughby as best I could, I went for help. I ran from the room to the stairs where the girl had descended earlier. Apart from help, I also decided on her capture and interrogation. What was her part in this monstrous business? What was in that infernal bucket?

Although without a candle, I took the first two stairs, and to my alarm, slipped to my back and clattered down the first flight. The stairs were both slippery and sticky. *What the deuce?* I thought as I tried to rise. I had this horrid liquid all over my clothes. Then I knew: it was blood! The characteristic iron smell I recognized was all over me. I ventured down the lower stairs gingerly as I had hurt my back in the fall above and wanted no further injury. Where was everyone? Why could no one hear the commotion? I gained the ground and looked around the inn and then again from top to bottom, calling out all the time. There was nobody, not a sign of life could I find. Even the stables were empty and showed little sign of recent occupancy. There were no servants housed above in the attic. No inn-keep. No daughter. It was just as if abandoned. Whatever, Willoughby and I were alive. However, this journal does not end yet. There is more, poor reader, and again I ask your forbearance in the telling and your prayers. How we made it back to civilization is of no concern. Just thank God that due to luck and the good offices of a local gentleman, we both made it to my aunt's house in Somerset, which, as it happens was not far from that cursed inn.

Willoughby's mind had left him, and he was unable to relate the events that befell him that night. At Lady Somerville's, my aunt's house, my friend was put to recover, if he ever could, from his stupor. His family was informed, and doctors attended him from London for regular bleeding; but nothing medical availed. It was decided by all that Willoughby should recover a little with us all here in Shropshire, and then stay with his cousin the Marquis of Maidstone in Kent. I, in shock, recuperated over some weeks but was never fully right. Now the uncanny part of my journal begins.

I could talk but little of the events at that inn from Hell. But some weeks later and after recovering somewhat, mention was made at a small dinner one evening by a certain Lady J of the district, who was dining with us, along with her husband. The dinner was cordial, considering the strangeness of the situation regarding my aunt's young relation and his friend, which had necessitated the canceling of all the usual season's social intercourse at the house.

"So, young Sir Humphrey, what perchance happened to you both? We're all agog to know." My aunt sighed and looked down at her fish, but she said nothing of the directness of this question and its inappropriateness at this time. I decided to finally relate events as I felt better, fortified by a little wine and broth—for I could hold nothing more. I started my story: the arrangements for New Year, the journey, the weather, the inn of the *Traveler's Respite* and all else besides up to our arrival. As you can well imagine, there was silence, but silence of an unexpected sort—and laced with more than just a little skepticism. The silence was broken by Lady J.

"That's a most marvelous story, sir, indeed. But I'm afraid quite wrong in fact. *The Traveler's Respite* is far from where you were found if Lady Somerville's account of your finding is correct. You must have made a mistake, young sir." She said this bluntly, but kindly.

I thought hard. Then I remembered the inn was not the *Traveler's Respite!* How stupid could I be? In my shock, I had confused one with the other. It was called *The Lamb!* Yes. *The Lamb!* I remembered the serving girl, the in-keep's daughter, telling us. I explained the confusion, but this then only fed more confusion. Faces stared at me; my fellow diners said nothing.

"Oh yes, it *was The Lamb!*" I insisted. "I remember the innkeeper's daughter saying it was a fine name for an inn that had saved so many souls. Or something like it." For a while back, I felt I was getting better but now not so.

"My dear boy, my dear boy, what know you of *The Lamb*?" questioned old Lord J. "For the inn of that name burned to the ground some years before our good King George took to the throne. For if *The Lamb* it is, a fateful and devilish tale is attached." I stared wide-eyed at him. The rest of the table stared wide-eyed at me.

Lord J spoke, "*The Lamb* was a good inn and its reputation for hospitality second to none about these parts. But there came one cold, stormy night a young Lord D and his knightly companion. They were given welcome of the warmest kind. But, as legend has it, the young Lord decided to sport with the innkeeper's daughter and did seed her with child that very night. The in-keep, when discovering this deed, became angry, but was prepared to forgive this carnal act and the betrayal concomitant if the young Lord married his daughter and recognized the child. A foolish request, of course. The Grim Lord D--for that is what we call him about parts here—refused. The in-keep then cursed him to the Devil, the Lord, and all aristocracy that would seek shelter and hospice from him.

"In time, the daughter bore a child. Now the Lord, enraged by the slight of the curse, rode with men to the inn one night. They did slaughter all and raze the inn to the ground. But first, he took the young baby and, breaking its bones, threw it down the well.

"But the Lord and his men did not live out the year. The curse upon them, in a twelve-month all were dead by some means or another. The Lord was thrown from his horse. He snapped his neck before the feast of Christ's Baptism had come. His companion died a year later, in mysterious circumstances, his body found frozen solid in the winter snow. The others I can't recall how they met their end."

When he had finished, we all sat in silence at this ghostly tale; I, finding my breathing difficult in my fear.

Suddenly a shrill cry was heard from above, and a tremendous crash emanated from Willoughby's convalescent room. As if as one, we all jumped up from the table, a couple of wine glasses toppling and a piece of cutlery clattering to the floor. We rushed up the long staircase—even old Lord J trying to climb it at a lick—to find Willoughby; there we did, but on all fours near the window, the curtains wide and blowing madly in the winter wind. He had clearly left his bed in some fever or whatever and was evidently alarmed beyond measure. He turned an ashen face to us and pointed out into the black night, struggling to speak. "Willoughby!" I cried. "What ails you, man?" To my horror, my friend from youth then produced what appeared to be a piece of a broken water-glass. Babbling something unintelligible, he plunged it deep into his neck. He fell forward on the floor, a jet of bright arterial blood shooting to the wall. He shuddered abruptly in his last throes, still pointing, and was dead in moments.

Dear reader, this journal is about to end. It is now a year on from those doleful events just described. I sit here after writing and look out from my library window into the cold crisp snow, which again has fallen hard this year. What supernatural events overtook us on the fateful journey? What conjunction of stars and planets changed our lives forever that night? For what greater cosmic purpose, if any? These are questions I have asked myself almost hourly over the past year as I await the inevitable call. I look from my window and… Ah! Yes, finally, it has come. There she is, waiting in the snow for me to join her. She's waiting for me, the fine buxom wench in the white night-shift. And she carries her well-bucket and in it her small broken baby, hanging loosely and dripping blood into the snow. I know I must go to her. I close my journal now, for my end has come—and may God have mercy on my soul!

Here Ends the Journal of Sir Humphry Valentine Cuthbert Hynde, Bart.

The Ninth Pyramid by Lee Clark Zumpe

When the Stalker among the Stars
Had but one Priest,
Here beneath the Ninth Pyramid
Schemed the Beast
To corrupt the frail minds of slaves,
Their dreams defile;
And to build a Wicked Empire
Along the Nile.

"Excuse Me, Sir, Is This a Joke?"
by
Christopher Dabrowski

As he did every day, Mark left his work at 1:30 p.m. to have a hot snack at a nearby lunch bar. When he left the cool interior of the office building, he was flushed by the heat of the sun. Blinded by sunlight, he blinked. For a few seconds, he just stood there, waiting for his eyes to get accustomed; suddenly, a feeling that something weird was going on overwhelmed him. He narrowed his eyes.

The street was full of non-moving cars.

"Such a traffic jam? Here?" He was surprised.

The drivers were getting mad and using their horns without any thought. They got out of their vehicles and looked around, uncertain. Some were listening to the radio news with real interest.

On the other side of the street, at a TV shop window, several dozen people were crowding. *Just like during a sale,* he thought.

It was only then, with a slight delay, when he heard tremendous noise from hundreds of radios and bleak grumbling of excited people.

What was going on? What was happening?

The first idea that came to his mind was that maybe it was another 9/11, but this time in Poland. A moment later, he envisioned a scene from the movie *Signs* where evil-minded flotillas of space ships from an alien civilization hovered over the biggest cities in the world.

He looked up at the sky. It was just like it always was, blue, spotted with peaceful fluffy clouds.

He ran the street, zigzagging between the cars and to the TV shop. Not without effort, he managed to squeeze through the excited crowd. Moments later, he could see the cause of this mess.

An ice-cold shiver ran through his neck, and his teeth chattered as if he had a fever. His heart pounded like a hammer, going faster and faster. Normally, he would be terrified. He would think that he had a premature heart attack, and he would have to pay the highest price for taking part in the corporative rat race. But now he just stood there, squeezed by the dense crowd, paralyzed with fear and yet fascinated by everything he had just seen.

"Excuse me, sir, is this a joke?" an old man standing next to him asked in a trembling voice.

At first, Mark didn't know how to reply. Woken up from a terrifying trance, he had a totally empty mind. If everything he saw was to be the end of everything, then the old man should be aware of that. He should be given time to accept the fact, get his life in order, pray, or ... in a blink of an eye, become a Buddhist believing in unification with a Higher Energy.

"This is not a film?" the old man asked, not believing his own eyes.

"Unfortunately, no," Mark replied.

The sky on the TV screen was spotted with black cubes.

What the hell was that? Did anything strange happen during the whole mad experiment with hadron collider? Maybe the scientists created an anomaly that was expanding at a terrifying pace and changing the molecules we know into units similar to itself, not known in our world.

You wouldn't call it "gaps in the clouds" either – you would have to see the stars, not just dead, impenetrable blackness. And those strange shapes ... maybe they were UFOs? The thing appeared so suddenly and out of nowhere. One moment there was a blue sky, a cloud, and then BOOM! Instead of a cloud, you had a tar-black cube.

****

A hysterical woman's voice shot through space, unbelievably high, making the skin on the back of Mark's neck tingle. He wanted to see what was going on, but he couldn't turn around; he was stuck in the human mass.

More screaming. Someone was praying aloud; another was laughing.

The pressure of the crowd got a bit smaller, and Mark could finally move. He looked up at the sky. There was a big black cube that mopped a part of a skyscraper up.

A real tornado arose inside the man's body. His heart pounded. Painful cramps gripped his stomach. The sweat from under his arms was flowing in steady, cold rivers, and the monotonous murmur in his ears was getting stronger. He started to feel weak, and he would faint if it weren't for the thought that banged through his head like a paper bag hit by a joker next to the ear.

Martha! Alicia! Oh, my God! Suddenly, he remembered that at the other end of the city, there were two terrified women. The meaning of his life. His wife and his daughter.

With a trembling hand, he reached for his mobile. His finger was oscillating like a drunkard with delirium, but he managed to find the right number. He pressed the phone to his ear. A few new cubes appeared in the sky. One of them gulped a plane that was flying by and covered the sun. The street was flooded with a dreadful shadow. In the speaker, Mark heard the message that the network was overloaded.

Fucking sure! He thought angrily.

He knew he must get to his family as fast as possible. He had to know if everything was okay where they lived. Considering the situation, no car was an option.

May he'd run? No, that's not possible. How could a man who smoked a pack per day run half a city like a doped marathon runner?

Mark was standing, helpless, throwing nervous looks at the area. Hit by chaotically running and screaming people, hurried by the increasing panic, he finally saw the solution. A second later, he was standing next to a boy leaning over a motor scooter looking to the sky with his mouth wide open. Mark pushed the boy and jumped onto the seat. The motor was running. Mark pressed the gas and took off, twisting and turning between the cars and the people.

Either it's the end of the world, or we are going to a different dimension. Either way, 1:0 for the damn Mayas, and the guy won't need his scooter after all. Mark excused his actions to himself.

He was on a sidewalk, free of the cars. Still using the horn, he zigzagged between the people who were jumping out of his way at the last moment. He didn't want to kill anyone by accident, just in case it would turn out that this was NOT the end of the world.

Everything got dark. The cubes were appearing as fast as the pimples on the face of a teen-ager. The city was flooded with dimness, with only a few columns of sunlight.

Mark was speeding the scooter as fast as he could. The cold wind was squeezing into his ears and freezing his dry throat, His eyes flooded with tears. He was risking his life; he could hit something or someone. But if he was more careful, he would not make it to Alice and Martha. He wouldn't whisper in a soothing voice that everything would be okay, although he would know that it wouldn't. They wouldn't hear for the last time that he loved them so much.

Or maybe this was just a dream? He was surprised that this had never occurred to him before, and that was his last thought. In a split second, his existence ceased. He disappeared in the nothingness of a cube that appeared in his way.

Mark was deleted from reality.

Place: the N'shaar planet. Time: before the end of the world.

N'shaar, a place so strange a human could hardly imagine it. A tar-black ball drifting in a milky white universe. From the outside, it looked dead, and indeed, its surface had no living organisms, but the inside ... that was different. It was full of life. With its vast hallways, it was sort of like a sponge. The tunnels were covered with giant ingrowths shining bright green light. These were the cities. In one ingrowth – in the city of Gaa'nth, preparation for a huge experiment was ending. On the edge of the city, in a zone adjacent to the tunnel surface, there was a laboratory complex HNAA'CS. Here, the most sophisticated technologies were developed.

A grey, blurred shape that was one of the inhabitants passed via mind blast a command to a bioter, that is, a specific computer that was about to create an artificial reality and artificial life.

A series of light blasts appeared. Scientists gathered in the room tuned their minds to be able to receive shape-thought beams. They didn't need any plots, descriptions, or photos; they experienced all their experiments via their sense of telepathy. Over the last few minutes, they got a massive transmission of shape-thoughts from the bioter. It indicated that the experiment would be a great success. Their minds explored the universe simulation and filtered billions of years of its existence. In a few substantial shape-thought blasts, they received knowledge about the artificial world.

It was a world where a life simulant was created – non-existing creatures that called themselves "humans." This world existed for a moment in a thousandth part of the last second of the experiment. Unfortunately, N'shaarians could not afford to continue the research. Sadness, cruelty, and all those terrifying feelings they received as a shape-thought transmission from the human planet were exciting yet scary. N'shaarians have never experienced anything like that as they simply didn't know such feelings, but they had to end the experiment. Based on their calculations, a few thousandths of a second later, the technical development of Earth would be at a dangerous level. There would be a possibility that the "humans" would learn to travel between the dimensions. This would mean that, theoretically, they could even invade the N'shaarian universe and become real material beings.

The human universe was deleted. The experiment was a great success.

****

The last moments of our universe: Earth. The USA. Stephen Winter's house in Los Angeles.

So finally, it happened. Stephen had known it for a long time. Thoughtfully looking into the vanishing reality, he wondered what the sense of it all was? Why did he bother and made a fool of himself trying to tell people the truth? Did it matter at all? What was the meaning of anything since it was known from the very beginning that Earth would end its existence? And of course, ... "existence" – a good one! Earth, the universe – that didn't happen at all!

When Stephen finished his study, when he saw the results, his hair went gray in a few seconds. He was terrified by what he discovered. The terrible truth. He was torn inside. For a few days, he was wondering whether he should keep the knowledge to himself or show it to the world. Finally, he decided that people had the right to know. And what was the end of it? Nothing! He was laughed at.

He announced that the universe and the reality around them were just a giant holograph, a sophisticated computer program. And they all took him for a madman; his greatest discovery became known as the largest bullshit in history.

Now, he was standing at the window, watching the hologram disappear, cube after a cube, cluster after a cluster, from the gods' hard drive.

On the one hand, this was sad – this feeling that you never existed, but yet, he felt great satisfaction. He knew that those who laughed at him had to change their minds and acknowledge his greatness and genius mind! It was a sad satisfaction. What do you need it for when you cease existing?

That's the end of everything, but wasn't it just what the humankind deserved?

The End

About the Contributors

Linda Barrett:

Ms. Barrett has been writing all her life. She wrote her first book at the age of eight. It's still in the McKinley Elementary school library. She was published in the *Huntingdon Junior Library* literary magazine by age thirteen. She's won three awards with the Montgomery County Community College Writer's contest. "Mr. Cat's Revenge" won third place in the 2014 MCCC contest. Ms. Barrett lives with her 84 years young mother in Abington in the same house for 50 years."

Rajeev Bhargava:

Rajeev lives in Harrow with his parents and five Chihuahuas. He has been writing since the age of twelve but had his first work published in 1990. Since then he's been writing stories, poems and articles for the small press as well as mainstream. His ambition is to be a freelance writer.

S. M. Bidwell:

S. M. Bidwell writes multi-genre now under three variations of her name. Given free rein, she veers to the disturbing with an undercurrent of the mysterious or unpleasant. The ability to write twisted tales has led to appearances in many publications. Longer works most notably include *Space: 1889*, and *Doctor Who* related fiction. Now living in the southwest of England, she hopes to write more stories that are dark, and gritty. She has lived in a house with a Harry Potter cupboard under the stairs, shared a publisher with the creator of *Roger Rabbit*, and once took a trip to Jupiter. Only one of these has been in her imagination. http://www.sharonbidwell.co.uk

Margaret L. Carter:

Reading *Dracula* at the age of twelve ignited Margaret L. Carter's interest in a wide range of speculative fiction and inspired her to become a writer. Vampires, however, have always remained close to her heart. Her work on vampirism in literature includes *Dracula: The Vampire and the Critics, The Vampire in Literature, A Critical Bibliography,* and *Different Blood: The Vampire as Alien.* She holds a PhD in English from the University of California (Irvine), and her dissertation contained a chapter on *Dracula.* In fiction, she has written horror, fantasy, and paranormal romance. Recent publications include *Crimson Dreams* (vampire romance), *Demon's Fall* (paranormal romance novella), *Heart's Desires and Dark Embraces* (story collection, fantasy and paranormal romance), and *Legacy of Magic* (sword and sorcery, in collaboration with her husband, Leslie Roy Carter). Her short stories have been published in anthologies such as the "Sword and Sorceress" and "Darkover" volumes, among others. "A Walk in the Mountains," co-written with her husband, appeared in the 2016 anthology *Realms of Darkover.* A sequel, "Believing," was included in *Masques of Darkover* (2017). Margaret's solo humorous ghost story, "Haunted Book Nook," appeared in the anthology *Sword and Sorceress* 33 (2018). She and her husband, a retired naval officer, live in Maryland and have four sons, several grandchildren and great-grandchildren, a St. Bernard, and two cats.

Francis-Marie de Châtillon:

Professional art historian and lecturer. Lives in North London and Florence. In long-term domestic partnership with a midwife. Enjoys country walks, swimming, and cooking with his partner.

Christopher T. Dabrowski:

Christopher has had numerous books published in the USA and Poland. His USA works include: *Anomaly* and *Escape*, both published by the Royal Hawaiian Press. Books published in Poland include *Anima Vilis* (Initium), *Grobbing* (Novae Res), *Deathbirth and other Stories* (Agharta & Amoryka), *Orgazmokalipsa*

(Alternatywne publishing house), *Anomalia* (Forma publishing house), and *Ucieczka* (2017 - Dom Horroru publishing house). Monika Olasek provided the English translation for his *Night to Dawn* stories.

Ruth Z. Deming:

Ruth Z. Deming has had her work published in venues including *Pure Slush, Literary Yard, Scarlet Leaf Review,* and *Creative Nonfiction.* This is her first story to be published in *Night to Dawn.* Ruth is a mental health advocate and runs *New Directions Support Group* of Abington and Willow Grove, PA.

Sandy DeLuca:

Sandy has written five novels; *Settling in Nazareth* (she painted the cover art), *Descent, Manhattan Grimoire, From Ashes,* and *Requiem for the Dead.* Her poetry chapbook, *Burial Plot in Sagittarius* (also created cover art and illustrations), was nominated for the BRAM STOKER award in 2001. Her art has been exhibited in galleries, hair salons, book stores and online venues. She has also painted covers and contributed interior illustrations for various numerous small press venues.

Chris Friend:

Chris has published his art in small press horror magazines for nearly 25 years. His surreal horror images have been featured in *Stygian Articles, Realm of the Vampire, Deathrealm, Black Petals,* and *Space and Time.* He draws his inspiration from Harry Clarke, H. R. Giger, and the horror comics of the 70s such as the Tomb of Dracula her and the Hammer Studios Frankenstein films. Chris friend can be reached at Mars_art_13@yahoo.com. Chris friend can be reached at Mars_art_13@yahoo.com.

To sample his illustrations, go to http://chris.michaelherring.net and http://www.moonlit-path.com/art-2-13-06.htm.

Todd Hanks:

The creative writing of Todd Hanks has been seen in publications such as Asimov's Science Fiction Magazine and the Kansas City Star newspaper.

David Harrington:

Originally from the East Coast, David B. Harrington has been a proud resident of Portland, Oregon since 1988. David enjoys playing Frisbee, tennis and the bass guitar occasionally. He also likes to read and write and his short fiction and poetry has been published in various magazines and anthologies both in print and online, including *Green Egg Zine, Journal of the Western Mystery Tradition, Hereditas; Dark Dossier Magazine, Schlock Quarterly, Lovecraftiana: Magazine of Eldritch Horror* from *Rogue Planet Press,* as well as *Sirens Call eZine, Spectral Realms from Hippocampus Press* and *Eldritch Tales* from *Necronomicon Press.*

Teresa Jay:

Originating from the UK but now residing in the Canary Islands, freelance artist Teresa Tunaley finds more time to devote to her love of art and painting. For years she has been doodling with pencils and dabbling with watercolors. More recently she uses a more modern technique and creates with her electronic tablet and pen in software such as Photoshop, Corel Draw and Paint Shop Pro. Along with published stories and poetry, she can be credited with award winning cover art and illustrations for author stories. Her work can be seen online and in print across the UK, US, Canada, Denmark and Europe. As Teresa put it, "I would like to think that I am very versatile in my choice of subject matter – my new surroundings provide the inspiration for me to paint on a daily basis and the fact that others may enjoy my work gives me the confidence to continue."

Website portfolio https://teresatunaley.wixsite.com/artstopper; E-mail post@artstopper.com

Tom Johnson:

Tom, a Vietnam veteran with twenty years in the military police (L.E.), has enjoyed literary success as a science fiction novelist with his action adventures in the Jurassic Period of Earth's predawn. He has created short story SF characters like Captain Danger of the *Space Rangers* and the galactic master thief, *The Forever Man* as futuristic space opera adventure. His many costumed crime fighters include two of his own creations, such as *The Black Ghost* and *The Masked Avenger*, as well as a western masked hero of the plains called *The Nightwind*. His latest is *The Man in the Black Fedora*. Sadly, Tom has passed away on November 4, 2019. His books are still available the websites are still open:

http://www15.brinkster.com/jur1/index.html

www.geocities.com/fadingshadows1/index.html.

Harold Kempka:

Harold's stories have been published in numerous magazines and ezines including *Night to Dawn, Blood Moon Rising, Black Petals, Inner Sins, Sanitarium, Yellow Mama,* and *Microhorror.* His horror short fiction anthologies, *Blue Plate Special* and *Discarded Treasures,* are currently available on Amazon Kindle, Barnes and Noble, and Smashwords, among others. *Discarded Treasures* is available in both paperback and e-book. Other anthologies including my stories are Pill Hill Press: Zombie Art Inspired Short Stories, Blood Bound Books: Seasons in the Abyss, and Post Mortem Press: *Shadowplay.*

Rod Marsden:

Rod Marsden hails from Sydney, Australia. He has three degrees related to writing and history. His stories have been published in Australia, England, Russia, the USA and now Canada. He has work in the American anthology *Cats Do it Better,* the American steam punkanthology *Break Time* and in the Canadian anthology *Morbid Metamorphosis.* Many of his short stories have been published in *Night to Dawn* magazine. His books include *Undead Reb Down Under and Other Vampire Stories, Disco Evil: Dead Man's Stand, Ghost Dance,* and *Desk Job* (his salute to Lewis Carroll). *Cold Water Conscience* is his venture into Crime/Horror. His short play, *Zombie Vision,* was well received at Cronulla Arts Theatre. His play *Hyde and Seek* was even better received. Rod has a fondness for Cronulla and the Wollongong area but an abiding love for the more northern Clarence River region of his home state of New South Wales.

Denny E. Marshall:

Denny E. Marshall has had art, poetry, and fiction published. Recent credits include cover art for *Bards And Sages Quarterly* Jan. 2017 and poetry in *Space And Time #126* Winter 2016. His flash fiction story "The Window" published by *Sci Phi Journal* is on the *Tangent Online 2016 Recommended Reading List,* a review magazine for short SF & fantasy. See more at www.dennymarshall.com

James Masters:

James was born in Tampa, Florida. When he was 16, his father died in an auto accident. This led to him moving to Ohio, and eventually, Parkersburg, West Virginia. He now works in Security and illustrates fantasy. He's been sketching since an early age and plans to send more illustrations to be featured in Night to Dawn.

Trisha Ridinger McKee:

Trisha Ridinger McKee resides in a small town that has its share of evening flea markets. Her work has appeared or is forthcoming in *Tablet Magazine, Crab Fat Literary Magazine, The Oddville Press, 4Star Stories, ParABnormal Magazine, Deep Fried Horror,* and more. Her work was recently nominated for the Best of the Net Anthology 2019.

Elizabeth Hattie Pierce-Collins:

Elizabeth first learned art and drawing from her mother. From there, she was self-taught until she was able to attend art school. She loves drawing the human figure and never stops studying the human body in motion. Her illustrations have appeared in *Night to Dawn* magazine and *The Spider's Web* (a novel). These have drawn positive attention from the readers. Elizabeth hopes to appear in more magazines and books in the future. For more information, contact Elizabeth at wackyursalinan45@aol.com.

Marge Simon:

Marge Simon's works appear in publications such as *DailySF Magazine, Pedestal, Dreams& Nightmares*. She edits a column for the HWA Newsletter, "Blood & Spades: Poets of the Dark Side," and serves as Chair of the Board of Trustees. She won the Strange Horizons Readers Choice Award, 2010, and the SFPA's Dwarf Stars Award, 2012. She has won three Bram Stoker Awards ® for Superior Work in Poetry, two first place Rhysling Awards and the Grand Master Award from the SF Poetry Association, 2015. In addition to her poetry, she has published two prose collections: *Christina's World*, Sam's Dot Publications, 2008 and *Like Birds in the Rain*, Sam's Dot, 2007. Her poems appear in *Qualia Nous* (Written Backwards), *The Dark Phantastique* (Jasunni Productions), Spectral Realms anthologies by S.T. Joshi, and more poems will appear in *Chiral Mad 3* and *Scary Out There*, a HWA/ Simon & Schuster Y/A collection, 2015. www.margesimon.com

Sravani Singampalli:

Sravani Singampalli is a published writer, poet and artist from India. Her works are published or forthcoming in many online and print journals and magazines. She is the winner of the Fiesta Love Poetry Competition 2018 and the 1st Submittable - Centric Poetry Contest. She was also one of the finalists for the Poetry Matters Poetry Contest and has won many prizes for her poetry. Her works were nominated for the Best of the net Anthology award by the Scarlet Leaf Review and the Spirit Fire Review.

Matthew Wilson:

Matthew Wilson has had over 150 appearances in such places as *Horror Zine, Star*Line, Spellbound, Illumen, Apokrupha Press, Gaslight Press, Sorcerers Signal* and many more. He is currently editing his first novel and can be contacted on twitter @matthew94544267.

Barry Yedvobnick:

Barry is a recently retired Biology Professor who performed molecular biology and genetic research at Emory University for 34 years. It has been his long-awaited dream to begin writing science fiction. He has not yet published a fiction story, but he has extensive nonfiction science writing experience, including 35 publications and reviews. Last June, he started writing a "Trends in Health" column for a local news-paper, *The Dahlonega Nugget*, where eight columns have appeared.

Lee Clark Zumpe:

Lee Clark Zumpe has been writing and publishing horror, dark fantasy and speculative fiction since the late 1990s. His short stories and poetry have appeared in a variety of publications such as *Weird Tales, Space and Time* and *Dark Wisdom;* and in anthologies such as *The Children of Gla'aki, Best New Zombie Tales Vol. 3, Through a Mythos Darkly, Heroes of Red Hook* and *World War Cthulhu*. His work has earned several honorable mentions in *The Year's Best Fantasy and Horror* collections.

As entertainment editor for Tampa Bay Newspapers, Lee has penned hundreds of film, thea-ter and book reviews and has interviewed novelists as well as music industry icons such as Paddy Moloney of The Chieftains and Alan Parsons. His work for TBN has been recognized repeatedly by the Florida Press Association, including a first-place award for criticism in the 2013 Better Weekly Newspaper Contest.

Lee lives on the west coast of Florida with his wife and daughter.

Visit www.leeclarkzumpe.com.

Meet the Corelli clan. Told by the oldest grandson, Frank, this family tapestry, with pathos and hilarity, begins weaving itself in the 1930s and rollicks through four riotous decades. The strongest thread is its oldest member, Antonio. To the ragtag Corelli clan, he is an ocean—an unwavering force upon which they rely. Lizzy, the youngest Corelli, is the brightest thread. Emanating from her is the light by which they see the world. Spanning these dynamic figures is an oddball cast of characters that keep one another in stitches right up until the life-affirming surprise birthday party of their beloved patriarch.

Night to Dawn Magazine & Books, LLC
www.bloodredshadow.com
www.amazon.com
www.bn.com

Author Tom Johnson

In a city of mob rule and crime, death is cheap, and police have their hands tied. In this dark metropolis, a new paladin arises to fight against injustice. A man of education, dedicated to fighting evil with fire against fire, the man in the black fedora.

www.amazon.com
www.bn.com